Grasshopper Speaks

Grasshopper Speaks

KATRINA M. REGISTER

Copyright © 2012 by Katrina M. Register
Copyright Number: 1-706467491

ISBN: 978-0-9851734-0-1

Contact the author at: Kat33003@aol.com

All rights reserved. No part of this publication may be reproduced, stored in a retrieval system or transmitted, in any form, or by any means, electronic, mechanical, recorded, photocopied, or otherwise, without the prior written permission of both the copyright owner and the above publisher of this book, except by a reviewer who may quote brief passages in a review.

The scanning, uploading, and distribution of this book via the Internet or via any other means without the permission of the publisher is illegal and punishable by law. Please purchase only authorized electronic editions and do not participate on or encourage electronic piracy of copyrightable materials. Your support of the author's rights is appreciated.

Printed in the United States of America

Acknowledgments

If there were stronger and more meaningful sentiments than *Thank You*, I would say them here. Yet, in the absence of such words, I say "Thank You" to all who understood, supported, and encouraged my need to take these thoughts from my soul and put them down in writing. And to her, him, and them – who provided the experiences, both happy and hurtful, I thank you as well. You have deliberately, or not, contributed to my story.

Preface

I thought I had the market cornered on hurt. Believing that no one else could possibly understand and/or relate to *my journey*. I buried my hurt, pain, frustration, fear, jealousy, and shame deep inside; in a place where I believed no one would find or recognize them. In my attempt to camouflage my demons, I became an expert at wearing masks. I had a mask for every day of the week, every situation, and every different person with whom I came into contact.

Most likely, you would have caught me in public with my head held high, shoulders back, designer names gracing my frame, and sashaying (as if to the tempo of my own theme music). But in the sanctity of my private space, I was insecure, naive, never sure of myself, always seeking the validation of others, and miserable from battling a never-ending series of internal conflicts.

There came a time when it became an increasingly

difficult burden to hide those internal torments that caused my spirit to ache. No amount of beautifying the outside could make pretty the ugliness that plagued what was on the inside. And no other person, material thing, money, or accomplishment could remedy my condition either. After a great deal of trial and error, I realized that the only person or thing that could make me well, whole, and joyous was me. God had provided me with everything I needed to initiate and achieve the task of becoming what I desired; it was up to me to put in the work and time to make it happen.

I began a process of self-therapy, which entailed reflecting on the significant relationships (familial, romantic, and professional) in my life, and understanding in what manner those interactions had contributed to the person I had become, and how they stood in the way of allowing me to become the person I wanted to be. I did not do this to place blame or to point the finger at anyone else. I did it, simply, to weed out those things that needed to be forgotten, to acknowledge what was worth remembering, and to identify what required me to forgive or to ask for forgiveness. This endeavor was bittersweet. Digging up old memories and experiences wasn't always pleasant; I shed many tears and was often tempted to give up working toward my objective. But I endured it and in the end was grateful that I did.

Writing my story was my therapy. And I thank you for reading it, because I desperately needed to tell it. I am sharing it because perhaps you will understand, relate in some way, laugh and cry with me, and maybe even use it assist in your own wellness. I am also sharing because I was in pieces – and I wished to be whole. I had allowed people and places to hold me hostage for far too long, and I needed my freedom. I had done things to others and myself, and I'd never accepted my share of the responsibility. And more than anything else, if I continued to play the role of victim, my children would inherit that trait from me. It is not what I desired to give them. And because I believe that we all have a choice in the direction of our journeys, hopefully, this therapy has changed mine – and will possibly change yours as well.

*For The Three
Whose lives I was Granted
the Gift of Being Caretaker:*

DJ, Ladybug, and Miss Kiy

*And there we saw the giants,
the sons of Anak,
which came of the giants:
and we were in our own sight
as grasshoppers,
and so were we in their sight.*

Numbers 13:33
-The Bible (KJV)

Book One

The Man in the Blue Suit

One day I met The Man in the Blue Suit.
Perhaps because of my need to both overly
    romanticize and analyze all things
I have afforded far too much credit to fate
for the joining of this union.
Maybe it didn't have a damn thing to do with
the alignment of the stars,
the fullness of the moon,
God's hands dealing the deck,
or the little, white slip of paper in the fortune cookie I
    had eaten the night before,
which read:
Love Awaits You.
Possibly,

it was simply a matter of he doing his business
and I doing mine,
and in the course of these events
I glanced into eyes deeper than I had experienced before.
The depth of love and pain that inhibited the man I saw in those weather-beaten windows
caused my soul to suffocate and my heart to momentarily stop beating and my mouth to barely open to formulate and utter the word, "Hello."
Quite conceivably,
Love at first sight
is a sham, a façade, a hoax – a belief that only the most foolish of fools could embrace.
And yet,
although my confidence in the existence of
the tooth fairy
the Easter bunny,
and a fat, white man, in a red outfit, with rosy cheeks sliding down my chimney on Christmas Eve to deliver beautifully-wrapped toys to peacefully-sleeping black children
had all been dispelled with the passing of childhood,
it is likely
that the one myth, I could not dismiss

is the one in which the handsome Knight In Shining
    Armor
comes to rescue the beautiful princess,
and they ride away on his magnificent steed
to the Kingdom of Love
and live happily ever after.

It is possible, I guess ...
Isn't it?

I thought it was him.
I was certain it was
The Man in the Blue Suit.

In afterthought
it seems I would have been better off continuing my
    belief in Santa Claus.
Little girls only cry for a short while when the doll
    with the curly hair isn't waiting under the tree.
The tears of a big girl, who continues her hope for
    the Knight, who simply can't or won't shine in her
    Kingdom

Flow
Unhappily
Ever After
And After
And After ...

Chapter One

"Grasshopper?"

The voice came from over my shoulder, which after connecting to my senses, rendered me immobile on impact and damn near caused me to choke on the sip of cranberry juice I had just taken. Although I had not heard that voice in over a year, there was no need to turn away from the airport bar where I had been lounging to confirm the identity of the speaker. I knew that voice well. It was the one I eagerly listened to – one that uttered words of guidance, motivation, and things a woman in love needed to hear.

Some evenings, after being rendered unconscious by the synthesis of he in me and one too many glasses of wine as well, I believed he had a tracking device implanted in my brain, which gave off signals when I was in trouble. Every time I was, my phone would ring

– and his voice would rescue me. Very melodramatic – but true, nonetheless.

That was when it was good. And then came the rain and the hurt and the bitterness – and the point relationships get to when the things you wish you could ignore snatch the blinders off your face – and everything is exposed for what it really has always been. And then you wish you could occupy any space in the world other than the spot where you are presently standing: that red circle clearly marked, in big, bold letters, called, "REALITY." And the voice, which was once that of an angel, is now one that you would swear in court belongs to the original Lucifer. Not the made-for-TV-one with the red, Lycra unitard and pitchfork. I'm talking about the for-real one that God kicked out of Heaven and who is running amuck, spreading his evilness all over the world. "Yes, your honor, I can make a positive identification; that's him, Lucifer, the man who assaulted and battered my heart."

In all fairness, I will not vilify him, nor will I allow anyone else to. Things happen, and usually two people contribute to those things. It would be less than an honest depiction of what happened, if I attempted to pass myself off in the matter as the innocent damsel in distress. It took some time to be woman enough to arrive at this conclusion.

At the onset of a love train-wreck, we women typically congregate with our girlfriends, sip wine and talk shit about how shitty men are. I suppose that when the heart aches, and we are welcomed into a comfort zone and granted the stage to play the grieving victim, it is easy to fool ourselves into believing we are replacing what we secretly yearn for: the perfect man, the perfect relationship, and the perfect home that is filled with two and a half perfect kids and a dog named "Perfect." But at some point, after you have starred in the lead role as victim for so long, the show goes into syndication and your viewing audience has dwindled down to only you; which may be a hint and a half to stop living in a re-run and start the process of understanding why your show keeps getting cancelled.

When my sitcom ended, I spent many sleepless nights staring into the nothingness of my dark bedroom. My only companion was the occasional glow from the headlights of a passing car, which managed to sneak past my curtains and disturb the prizefight that was underway in the solitude of my room. No spectators, announcer, or cameras – just me in one corner, facing off, against me in the other corner. The bell would sound and I would come out whipping my ass.

Guilt is a funny thing. On the one hand, it provides you with the reality of your imperfectness, and forces the guilt-ridden party to reflect upon what was done, the manner in which it was done, why it was done in this manner, and why it would be most prudent not to commit the same offense again. On the other side of the spectrum, guilt is pure self-mutilation. Once the act is committed, the ugly words spew out, and diabolical deeds are done, no amount of kicking your own butt will erase any of it. Guilt is not admirable. Seeking redemption – yes. Seeking forgiveness – yes. But guilt allows no room to redeem or forgive oneself. It just hangs around like a boulder attached to your neck. And if nothing is done to rid yourself of this albatross, it feeds off your soul. It suffocates your inner-being to the point where breathing is such a tremendous task, that the guilt-bearer may find herself imprisoned in periods of surrender – when she'd rather retreat, throw up the white flag, and let the freaken albatross win the war, rather than to continue to engage in a senseless series of battles. I was almost there.

One late night, about a year ago, I entered into my final conflict with Guilt. Although we had waged war on numerous occasions, this time was different; he brought some friends along with him. Thinking back, I suppose they had always accompanied him, choosing to obscure themselves from my view. This time, I detected them as soon as the skirmish was in motion.

Shame was the opponent I spotted first. She was smiling as if she were already aware of what the outcome of this fiasco would be. And why shouldn't she be so certain of herself? It was always Shame who could reduce me to feelings of worthlessness. It was this heifer that never hesitated to show up and show out when I felt good about some accomplishment, or myself. And she was always so very congenial about helping me step down from my bandwagon, while reminding me that I was some whore's abandoned child, and that I have three children by three different men, and that everything I had ever accomplished had been done to earn some validation, some love, and some semblance of anything that resembled pride from a mother who seemed more annoyed with my existence than anything else. Yes, based on our prior dealings, Shame had great reason to smile.

Even if I could have managed to take on both her and Guilt, I figured there was no way in hell that I could handle them and their associates: Fear, Resentment, Jealousy, Pride, and Bitterness, who were standing there – dressed in full battle regalia – looking at me like, "What Up Playa?" I might be from Newark, but I do understand when it's time to count your losses and haul ass! White Flag!

As they closed in, my doom was imminent; but as any great warrior, I decided to die at the hands of my own sword, not theirs. I remember sitting on the floor, crying and praying – praying and crying. At the time, I was certain that God could no longer hear me. It seemed as if He had: stopped taking my calls and had changed His home, cell, and business numbers; e-mail address; and place of residence to make me get a clue that He was no longer available to me.

At some point, I moved to stand in front of the bathroom mirror, holding the full bottle of Percocet that the doctor had prescribed to alleviate discomfort from the miscarriage. As I began to twist the top off the bottle of Vodka, which had recently become a frequent visitor to my nightstand, it dawned on me that my fifteen-year-old daughter was asleep in the next room, and that I needed to write a letter or something, to her and my other two children, to explain why Mommy did what she did.

I found a notebook and a pen and began drafting my exit letter. First draft: *Dear Children*, - ripped that sheet up to begin again. Second draft: *My Beloved Children*, -

balled that one up and threw it so hard I thought I had broken my wrist. Third and final draft: *To You Whom I Gave Life*, - now this one got me. I sat there, absorbed in the truth of what I had written: *I had given someone life. I had brought three human beings into creation. God had entrusted ME with that weighty responsibility. Who would take on that charge if I wasn't there?*

Then I thought: *Dammit, let their fathers do it. I've done more than my share ... But I would like to see their lives unfold ... be there for back-to-school nights and recitals and sports competitions and graduations and first romances and Mommy advice and Mommy hugs and Mommy kisses ...*

I placed the now infamous six-word suicide note in the Bible that was collecting dust (and stains, due to the lack of fine motor-skills of an occasional drunken hand). Then I walked to my daughter's room, opened the door, and admired her from the doorway (as if she were a rare, precious gem in a glass case that I desired to have and hold - yet one that I neither knew how to obtain nor deserved to possess). I stood there for a half-hour or so, thinking of them: the three whose lives I had been granted the gift of being caretaker. I would not throw my gifts in God's face. I could not leave. Not like this. Not now – not ever.

Afraid to re-visit my bedroom, for fear that my demons (whom I'm sure were pissed by their triple-overtime, unexpected defeat) might still be lurking and plotting revenge, I positioned myself in a small space at the foot of my daughter's bed. I slept there with her that night, abundantly grateful that she, her brother, and sister had saved my life.

Chapter Two

Now, twelve months later, there I was – waiting for the announcement of my delayed flight, accosted by the voice of the man who had entered my life by chance, kidnapping my heart, soul, and flesh; and filling every part of my being with vast paradoxes of love and hate – joy and pain. I'd done all that was humanly possible to keep my distance from him. After the miscarriage, I had changed my phone number and deleted him as a friend on mutual social networks. It wasn't his style to come to my home uninvited. And because we lived in two different regions of the state, I wasn't concerned about running into him.

Actually, the miscarriage had happened on a Sunday. I had made communication changes the following Thursday after Coach had called and texted during the preceding three days. I simply, or not so simply, didn't know what to say.

That was a first in our three-year liaison; because the essence of what we did was share words. Intellectual words; motivating, supportive words; loving words; bitter, angry, hurtful words; our connection centered on words. I had felt an indescribable emptiness the moment I had realized that our words had run their course. We had, I believe unintentionally, used all the words up. If there had been the possibility of purchasing more words, somewhere – anywhere, I would have spent my last penny to attain them. Unfortunately (or not) that which is most precious cannot be bought or sold.

At the hospital, on the Sunday that the miscarriage had occurred, I lay in the examination room of the ER, frozen, staring up at the light that was way too damn bright to illuminate the room of a sick person. I cringed as I analyzed the mental raw-footage of the last two hours.

The video began in church. I, rushing in – late – was ushered to an empty seat, and went to the innermost vacant space on the pew. I took off my coat, laid down my handbag, and pulled out my Bible. I whispered to the woman next to me, "Can you tell me what scripture we're reading?"

She gave me that, "If you had your ass here on time you would know which scripture we were reading – but

I'm going to be a good Christian and point my well-manicured finger to the passage, and hopefully you will see what I pointed to – 'cause I don't have time for your nonsense; I'm trying to praise my Jesus" look.

I smiled, reluctantly and sarcastically replied, "Thank you, saint."

But long before I had gotten the "you" out, she had already rolled her eyes and looked away, dismissing the annoyance of my intrusion in her worship space. I had just joined in the reading of Mark 9:42, "And whosoever shall offend one of these little ones that believe in me …" when I felt a tap on my shoulder, as if someone had something urgent to relay. I turned to face the messenger and was greeted by the grimaced and worried expression of the woman in the pew behind me. She informed me, as gently and quietly as possible (while competing with the volume of the congregational scripture reading), "There's something red all over the back of your skirt, dear."

Next came the barrage of post-intelligence events. In one movement, I shielded my exposed business behind the security of my outerwear, grabbed my purse and Bible, and fled the sanctuary. I was successful in escaping to my vehicle without my blood-soaked skirt being revealed to any more of my fellow parishioners, but I was far from being out of harm's way.

Once in the car the abdominal cramps began, followed by the sensation of blood clots exiting my womb, which were absorbed by my car seat. The only thing I could think to be grateful for was that my girls had won their protest to skip church to attend their cousin's sleepover; all else seemed bleak. My dramatic entrance into the hospital parking lot, some twenty minutes later, was preceded with an even more theatrical trip there, filled with the silent pleading and bargaining we tend to do with God when we know we have officially messed up.

When I finally surfaced in the ER – half walking, half running – the scene was surreal. It was as if I had made my appearance on stage, without my script, or any understanding of what was expected of me or from the rest of the cast.

The plot of the storyline had come into creation four weeks prior when I had texted Coach on that Saturday morning to let him know that I was coming down to purchase the golf membership that he had hinted he wanted for his birthday. I had gone back and forth, debating my decision to buy the membership from the moment he had mentioned it. Already feeling taken for granted, coupled with the fact that he had recently announced that he had a "friend," had made the decision to give such an expensive gift, one for serious consideration. After a great amount of deliberation, the verdict was in: I loved Coach – Coach loved me. We didn't have an exclusive relationship, and because I had moved an hour away, we hadn't really seen each other, so that other girl was just a fill in, because he missed me. Besides, I wanted to make him happy; giving him the golf membership would make him happy. Case closed …

Wondering whether I am too old to LOL and SMH at myself? Now, I can actually do both when I think about the way I would fool myself into justifying the things I did with Coach. The truth of the matter is I, as many fools in love do, had been playing a game – a competition of sorts – one for which I did not know the rules and had not been given the instruction manual. So, I had put my sneakers on and had been running in circles – quite the way a hamster runs on its wheel – expending a great amount of time and energy, yet never reaching a destination. That was me with Coach: the hamster on the wheel.

> *Being willing, without anger, to acknowledge the foolish things we've done is the first step to healing.*

I loved him though – as best as I could. The problem was that I didn't love myself enough to play the love game with Coach or anyone else. Two marriages, one engagement, and Coach, and I still did the same thing the same way. My picture should be placed next to the definition of insanity in the dictionary. Through my many flawed attempts at having a productive relationship, it had never occurred to me that I was in pieces.

A productive, meaningful relationship requires two whole people, not one, or none. It takes a whole person to love someone in a manner that doesn't require sacrifice of the parts of you that are necessary to continue to love yourself. How do you love someone else more than you love yourself? In being whole, I believe, you understand how much of yourself to give, why you give, when to fall back, when to come forward, when to keep going, and when to stop. In my case, in addition to being in pieces, I was in a state of something akin to an addiction that would not allow me to walk away from this man. This dependence, complicated by my ego, compelled me to keep running on that wheel.

These factors led me to Coach that Saturday afternoon. I – bearing gifts; he – pleased. I made Coach smile. Great job, Grasshopper! That smile was priceless to me – and worth every dollar spent on this very impressive token of my affection, that both of us knew I couldn't easily afford. Might I at this time re-iterate my defense? A Fool in Love.

Mutual smiles led to explicit flirting, which led to an impromptu excursion to our favorite gambling destination. I loved those brief get-a-ways with him. It was our private space – our own little world. I was safe there; my soul was free there. Above all else, Coach was there, and nothing else mattered.

When out and about on our fantasy island interludes, I was fascinated by the way others viewed the interactions between Coach and me. When mingling with strangers, it was clear that they assumed we were a happy couple. I wouldn't say a word, but Coach always played right along with the charade. To others, we appeared a perfect depiction of the Joneses; a handsome pair: degreed professionals, well-spoken, well-outfitted; out on a date night, having left the kids, the house and dog in the capable hands of Grandma Jones.

Appearances can be deceiving. We were not a couple – nor had we ever been. My desire to have an exclusive relationship had been a point of contention for almost the entire stretch of our three-year, on-again, off-again situation. The end result of every "relationship" conversation was always the same; I knew, verbatim, the dialogue that would come from those less-than-pleasant chats:

Production Title:

Push and Pull: The Chronicles of Grasshopper & Coach

A Two-Character, One Act, One-Scene Play

As the act begins, Grasshopper is lying on a bed and has just telephoned Coach. She is visibly nervous and anxious.

Coach: (*answering the phone*) What's going on Grasshopper?

Grasshopper: (*unable to verbalize her thoughts*) I … I … um … well, I … I mean … you know I love you, and … I think – maybe – it's time to –

Coach: (*now agitated, cuts Grasshopper off*) Don't do this … shit is cool. Why do we need to revisit this now?

Grasshopper (*flustered, losing her fight to hold back the tears*): I just thought –

Coach: (*more agitated*) That's what happens. You start just thinkin' and we start beefing. Nothing has changed since the last time you were just thinkin'. I'm not ready. Stop trying to lead me down a road I don't want to be on!

Grasshopper: (*defeated*) I can't do this anymore.

Coach: (*exasperated*) So don't! Why does it always have to be all or nothing with you? Every time you try to draw a fucking line in the sand – you already know you'll be on one side by your damn self! I don't have time for this shit, man! Do you, Grasshopper! Peace and Blessings!

(*The call is disconnected. As the curtains closes, Grasshopper balls into a fetal position, covering her entire body with the comforter.*)

I saw that play. Two thumbs down – hated it!

The same production played itself out, over and over again. Same script. Same characters. I remained. I figured maybe one day, when he was ready, I would be granted the keys to the kingdom and have it all. I artfully conned myself into believing that I had something, which was better than having nothing. Me: the silly, little hamster on the wheel. In reality, not only did the loving Joneses not have a home, I had never been invited inside his residence. All I knew of his children were their names. I assume he didn't have a dog, because he never mentioned one. But then again, why would he need a dog? He had a loyal pet hamster.

This particular excursion, our last, ended with several nightcaps and sex. We so infrequently had sex that it almost came as an unnecessary interruption of "our thing' when it did happen. Not saying it wasn't good; homey put in work. And I was a master of his body. I knew every caramel- flavored inch of his toned physique. But there was no need for him to cradle my breasts, or kiss there or there, or part my limbs and invade my privacy; all of that was extra. The intimacy I enjoyed most with Coach was when he made love to my mind and spirit – the power of words.

Our best words were shared over evening cocktails

or at Barnes and Noble on mid-afternoon Sundays – debating and politicking over books, ideologies, and his career or mine. Not to mention the marathon phone conversations we would have after some great injustice had befallen me, and I would seek his guidance for a strategic action plan. That's how our nicknames developed. He called me "Grasshopper" and I called him "Coach." He was the instructor – I, the eager student.

I became dependent on those roles. Even when I could easily have figured out some meager challenge for myself, I still called on him. When some new development in the life of Grasshopper occurred, he knew first. And when there was nothing in particular to report, I have, on occasion, been guilty of conjuring some happening, just to receive the benefit of Coach's full attention. He liked being "Coach" – the leader – the one who seemingly thought for two people. I had no problem being Grasshopper – the follower – the one who couldn't tie her own shoe without his assistance. I figured he knew I was intelligent and strong. Allowing the light to always shine on him didn't take away from my star, did it? Sometimes hamsters run in the dark.

In retrospect, I wish we had skipped the co-mingling of bodies that evening. But we didn't. In the midst of that physical act, a child was conceived and his parents significantly shortened the plan for his life. After numerous heated debates, Coach reigned as the victor. I remember our exchange, (after the missed period) as I paced the hallway outside the gynecologist's office, awaiting the test results.

"Coach, give me one good reason why I should have an abortion."

"I can give you more than one, Grasshopper. For one, I told you before that I didn't want any more children. Two, you're in grad school and trying to make moves in your career. Three, I'm not in that place. Things are progressing in my career. My focus is on my children and career; you knew that already."

I muttered, "Okay" and hung up the phone.

How do you fight that? He had a point; I did know. Coach wins. I prayed that by some stroke of luck, the goodness of the universe, or the grace of the Almighty, that the results would be negative. But the plus sign confirmed that the leprechaun had abandoned me as well. Game played; I lost. I had been running and running on that damn wheel, with no evident indication of a finish line. I had fought for his time, his affection, his attention, and his love. In my palm, I held on tightly to the possibility of his seeing something – anything – in me that would make me worthy of being a significant

Chapter Two

partner in our "Joneses" equation. I finally unclenched my hand to find nothing there but dust. I had no fight left. I climbed down off the wheel and unlaced my track shoes.

Before I had the dreadful opportunity to walk inside the clinic, lie down on the table, place my bare feet in the stirrups, and have the doctor administer something into my veins that would render me unconscious of the removal of the life – the unwanted gift – that was being returned to the Giver of Life – nature decided to return the child in its own way.

So on that Sunday morning, after fleeing from church, I made my entrance onto the stage, cast in the starring role. My supporting cast included the nurse at the reception desk, who, perfectly on cue, looked up from her computer, saw the agony on my face, as well as, my blood-drenched garments, and immediately rushed from behind her post and ushered me into triage. The triage nurse took my vitals and provided me a gown and a sanitary napkin (so long I could have wrapped it around my head at least twice). Both the attending nurse and physician added stellar recurring performances, as each in their respective roles gently asked the, "I'm sorry to have to ask this …" questions; and performed the, "I'm sorry to have to do this …" examination. The ultrasound tech was a minor character, whose un-dynamic role ended after he applied the cold gel on my stomach, rolled the little ball attached to his instrument of trade, and viewed the white, black, and grey areas on the screen. A few clicks of his computer mouse and his scene ended.

As I was wheeled back to the exam room, I thought for a brief moment, to call Coach. In that moment I realized that all the words had been used up. I was empty and angry. Bitterness began its descent on my spirit. I purposely decided to hate him with all the venom I could produce. Acting career over. Not coming back on this stage again.

After a few months, the anger eventually subsided and morphed, interchangeably, between guilt and a longing for Coach. One moment I was in the ring, jabbing and upper-cutting myself for being such a fool. The next moment I desired to hear him speak. I replayed over and over again the first time I heard his voice. It wasn't a magical moment – just him doing his job and me doing mine. Perhaps our meeting was a matter of Fate toying with the puppets under his control. Who can ever be sure of why or how people come into your life? What their function will be? Whether they will be

Chapter Two

a benefactor who contributes greatly to your existence or the bitch or bastard you wish you'd never met?

In regard to Coach, I have yet to determine these answers. I know he helped me in some ways, and annihilated me in others. My view of the situation is often biased by my present temperament and disposition. The fact is that he offered what he could give: advice, encouragement, inspiration, motivation, intellectual discourse, and some very good moments. His heart, his feelings, and his desire to fall in love were unavailable, so those were not proffered. Those things belonged to him, and those who attempted to tread past the barbed wired gates and the well-armed sentry to gain entry to the recesses of the frigid dungeon where he safeguarded his prized-possessions, did so at their own demise.

Had I been privy to this information from the onset of our first meeting, perhaps I would have refused the invitation to discuss my dilemma in his office and remain there conversing with him until it had been rectified. Possibly, I would have declined his offer to visit my place of employment later that afternoon and have him offer suggestions as to how to remedy what I considered a pressing situation. Then there would have been no continuing dialogue, or exchange of cell phone numbers, or the thinking, "he has potential" after the evening telephone call, or the lunch date the following day, or the dinner date the following night, or my biting of the pillow to muffle the effect of his initial admittance into my sacred places – which proceeded dinner, or that hazy-floating-can't-believe-I-really-did-that-shit-but-loved-every-second-of-it space during the morning-after breakfast. The forty-eight hours – he had me, smitten as hell. He was a stranger, but I believed his eyes. His eyes ensured that it was okay. In another time and place maybe it would have been. But, he wasn't ready and neither was I.

Chapter Three

Daddy had died a year earlier and a significant part of me was sealed in his casket and buried with him. Daddy was everything that daddies are created to be: protector, provider, a little girl's first love, and the foremost man whom she respects and admires. I know people have a tendency to embellish a person's life after they have died. But as God was my witness, Daddy was one of the best men who ever walked this earth. He was kind and giving and loving. He enjoyed sharing a good story and a hearty laugh.

He took care of his home and everyone in it – even when our appreciation for it was less than he deserved. If you caught him out, likely he was on his way to or from work, church, lodge meeting, or some countless task that involved his wife and/or children. If he ever had a side honey, she knew her position and played it well; I never heard arguing involving an indiscretion on his behalf, and no woman was ever brazen enough to call our home phone or show up at the front door. He did flirt and was fond of being flirted with. But my best guesstimate is that his attraction to other women, or theirs to him, was left at a look, a grin, or speaking – but don't touch; which, for him or anyone else, I find reasonable. It's the acting on the attraction that tends to jack things up.

Outside of the ego flirting (which is what I call it), I can only think of two other flaws that Daddy had. The first: the light-skin/dark-skin thing. Daddy was dark: black-black. To me, his skin was beautiful. To him, it served as a reminder of being the nigger who damn well better avert his eyes to the ground when dealing with a white person; and the nigger who may find himself hanging in the tree like the nigger over yonder if he had a mind to ever get uppity and forget his place; or the nigger who resided in the proximity of other niggers, who all attended the same nigger schools and nigger church and nigger doctor at the nigger hospital, and would sweat alongside each other to plant and cultivate 100 percent of some crop from which they would only reap ten percent of the proceeds.

And after everyone, including other niggers, verified that being black was tantamount to being nothing

Chapter Three

worthy, I suppose he believed it, too. Yet, more so than that, he signed up for and became a believer in the "White and Light is Right Theory": the train of thought that promotes the belief that the next best thing to being a white person is being a light-skinned black person. Daddy would only hire white plumbers or electricians or contractors to do work in our home. He had white doctors and a white financial consultant. Daddy would say that Negroes were shiftless, lazy, and couldn't be trusted.

When I arrived at the age to debate with my father without the fear of being punished or spanked, we had more than a few arguments on this topic. I relentlessly tried to persuade him to understand that his beliefs were no more than the propaganda and brainwashing that he had inherited from the society in which he had been raised. But Daddy had no use for my socio-psycho-political ranting, and kept right on using his skin-bleaching cream and holding all that was white or light in high esteem.

My mother would accuse Daddy of favoring me because I was light; I figured she was mad that she wasn't, and I dismissed her and her nonsensical speculation. Yet, it is plausible that there was some truth to her theory. I would have never given her the satisfaction of admitting it for two reasons, though. First, the implications of this would completely undermine my perception of my relationship with Daddy and diminish our paradigm of the model father and daughter into a man's foolish fancy of his little house nigger, rather than a sincere love for his child. Second, I had no desire to give away the one thing that belonged to me. Daddy's love was the only good thing I had; and I refused to lose it. Period.

Daddy's other flaw was that he became bitter about the pastor of our church. In three words or less: Daddy hated him. I had never known my father to show blatant malice toward anyone, but this man was (in his mind) his arch-nemesis. The new pastor had come to our church after the passing of a man who was not only the spiritual leader for forty-years, but he was also Dad's well-respected and trusted surrogate father. He was also part of a fading era of the old-school church, prior to the creation of the mega-media church.

Daddy was a stranger to the charismatic, political, affluent persona that now resided in the pulpit of the church where he had worshiped for more than four decades. He decided, from the door, that this dude was a crook who wasn't to be trusted. But, the pastor's lovely wife and kids, and their lovely Neiman Marcus clothes, and their lovely cars and lovely home out in the lovely

Chapter Three

suburbs (which was off limits to the sheep) won over the majority of the flock, including me.

We were enamored by their lives. They had lives we wished we had. Or rather, they had things and the appearance of the lives we wished we had. My mother was so caught up in the hysteria of her new pastor that she often bragged that she was on the committee that cleaned his study. For my father, I believe, my mother's obsession, in some crazy way, meant competition with another man.

Mother's awe of this man, coupled with an admiration and devotion that was never shown to my father, caused Daddy to show pastor the same jealously and wrath that would have been extended toward a man that Mom was sharing her bed and goodies with. I wish it were as simple as that. Many can forgive a cheating spouse, who caught in moments of temptation and desire, selfishly barter their body as a temporary substitute for what's missing at home. But how do you forgive a woman, to whom you have committed most of your adult life, when she says things like, "That man got more sense in one finger than your dumb-ass got in your whole black-ass body"? What man could tolerate that?

My brother and I did the best we could to remain as far away from that debacle as possible. But our attempt at being mutually neutral allies was futile. Within a ten-year span my mother and father's holy war affected everyone in our home. Even my children and my brother's daughter were conscious of the carnage that would result from mentioning anything about church. In the midst of a holiday celebration, a child's birthday party, a barbecue, or one of the kids' recitals or sports competitions, the slightest innuendo or reminder of church was enough to ruin an event. And my parents, who had rarely fought about anything, would viciously attack each other.

C'mon, about church? I thought church was meant to bring people – families – closer together. Church, somehow, destroyed my family and left it in ruins. What it also did was turn me against organized religion. The manner in which people treat religious figures as demi-gods sickens me. In my estimation, they are human, like the rest of us. But we'll write a check for $1000 for the Pastor's Anniversary; then scrape, avoid collection calls, and pray the lights don't get cut off before we can pay the debts that should have been satisfied with that money. And God forbid that the pastor should get caught with his hand in the cookie jar or up someone's cookie. Life, as we know it, is over. Wrong or right, and a bit jaded, I have become more interested in my

Chapter Three

relationship with the Being upstairs, rather than the ones who stand up the velvet stairs in the pulpit.

Regardless of his faults, Daddy was and will always be my hero. My fondest memories of my childhood are those that were shared with him. As a young girl, the times I most enjoyed with Daddy were spent sitting on his lap at the kitchen table. I read – he listened. He asked questions – I answered them. I became Daddy's reader early on. Having grown up in the South during a time when someone deemed it more important for little, black boys to share-crop than attend school, his education had been intermittent; and the high school diploma he eventually received from the State of Alabama wasn't a true testament that he was proficiently instructed in reading, 'riting, and 'rithmatic, because Daddy was functionally illiterate.

Of course I wasn't aware of this as a child, but it wouldn't have mattered to me if I had known. From the time I could read, I sat on Daddy's lap and read the newspaper, documents, and anything else that needed to be interpreted. Being his reader was a special position for me. This was my time with Daddy. Him needing me to help figure out what some form meant was a small price to pay for all he provided. I'm sure there were times that an impatient twelve-year-old, who longed to join a kick-ball game or a double-dutch competition on a summer day – or the busy twenty-year-old, whose adult life was beginning to bloom into an identity of its own – was resentful of having to be held up or slowed down by reading for Daddy. But, all in all, I enjoyed being the bridge between Daddy and the world of words.

I suppose it was a good thing that Daddy boarded a bus in route to New Jersey when he did. His character and work ethic gained him a permanent position as a longshoreman (he called it "the last of the muscle jobs"). He loved that job. He went to work sick. He went to work tired. Sometimes he worked for days at a time, sleeping at the port – returning home for a good meal, hot bath, and the opportunity to rest in his bed. When the alarm clock announced 4:45 AM – the start of a new day – Daddy never hit snooze or lingered under the warmth of the covers. He rose, prepared his breakfast and lunch, and was back to the grind.

Yet, as much as he worked, there was not a time that I can recall him missing a school concert, dance recital, or music lesson. He was also the official point person of transport to and from friends' homes, the mall, and work. During my freshman and sophomore years of undergrad, my friends and I would wait impatiently for

Chapter Three

the tan Delta Eighty-Eight to arrive on campus. I'm sure Daddy's appearance meant something entirely different for my girlfriends than it did for me. For them, it was a ride home or the chance to spend the weekend away. For me, my father was in my presence. I could see him, kiss his cheek, and hug his neck – the things I longed to do during the time that I was three hours away from home and infrequently heard his voice on the phone.

There were four of us in our home – but Daddy and I were the closest two. Extended family such as grandparents, aunts, uncles, and cousins were methodically denied access to my brother and me –or maybe more so from me. Daddy found, early on, that the intolerance and contempt that my mother's family and some members of his, showed toward John and Mary's two adopted kids (especially the little, yellow girl) was something we needed protection from. So it was the four of us: Thanksgiving dinner, Christmas dinner, Sunday dinner, every other dinner, and every other day – just us.

My brother was more involved with the happenings in the neighborhood; and my mother was more concerned with girlfriends, sisters, and whatever else it is that women who are not satisfied at home are prone to be interested in. That left my father and me up to our own shenanigans. The two of us spent countless hours on the living room couch watching baseball, basketball, and football. We did the grocery shopping together, a task he most likely would have preferred to do without me – given that I was compelled to have everything in the store, and he felt duty-bound to buy it for me. If we went somewhere at night, I would conveniently fall asleep just minutes prior to pulling into the driveway. He would lift me out the car and carry me upstairs to our apartment. At some point, I'm sure he figured this little ruse out, but we continued this practice until I was too old and too heavy to carry up the flight of stairs.

Daddy would come home exhausted, but he would swing me in the air and spin me around until I was laughing so hard that I had to beg him to stop. And how could I not mention that my father loved to see me dance? I started dance training as a toddler and continued, in some capacity, until I was thirty-seven. Daddy rarely missed a performance.

And so it was with Daddy and me. He was my best friend, protector, provider, and biggest cheerleader. He was the one who said, "I'm proud of you" for even the smallest of accomplishments. And I did everything I could to make him proud. It wasn't until my freshman year of college that I brought the first major disappointment his way. I met a boy during the second week of school who, soon after, became my boyfriend, and three months later became the father of my first child.

When I found out I was pregnant, the last person on the planet I intended to tell was my dad. It was his hard-earned money that allowed me to remain a stranger to the never-ending financial aid lines. I had eavesdropped from the next room as he called his friends and relatives to report, "I'm taking my baby to school tomorrow!"

And I had seen the look on his face as he brought the last of my belongings into my dorm room, struggled to find the words to say, and instead hugged me until I understood all he needed to say from his embrace. He had kissed me on my forehead and left. I had cried, watching the Oldsmobile drive away. I had wondered whether he cried too, or whether he uttered a few words to God, asking Him to protect me in his absence. How could I tell Daddy?

My girlfriends had already provided their expert opinions on the matter.

"Why would you have a baby? ... Especially by him!"

"You know he messes with other girls, Trina!"

"And soon as you tell him – he's gonna dis you!"

And on – and on. I was the hot topic of conversation. Not that my friends weren't screwing around too (by every stretch of the imagination they were); but I was the only one contemplating the notion of allowing a child to be produced from my lustful, sneaking into the boy's dorms after curfew, nights.

Chapter Four

"A baby? C'mon, Trina! What the hell are we gonna do with a baby? Shit – we're in college! … And your fucking father hates me! That muthafucka is gonna bust a vein when he finds out the little princess is pregnant! ... Naah, man … Naah … I'll see if I can get some money from my parents … You know I'll go with you, Trina … What the fuck are you crying for? … You shouda been on the pill or something! … If you're gonna keep that fucken crying up – just get the fuck outta my room!"

That was the extent of the first pregnancy conversation. Over the course of the next twenty years, I would experience conversations similar in context three more times – with three different men. "All book smart and no common sense" is what my brother has always said of me.

On the day of the scheduled termination, he and I rode in his car in silence. At some point he switched on the radio, only to immediately switch it back off again after hearing the refrain of "Thanks for my Child." When we arrived at the clinic, he parked the car, turned it off and remained motionless. I assumed this was my cue to get out. I did so, and began walking toward the entrance, glancing behind me once to see if he had decided to join me. He didn't.

I did my best to keep a steady hand as I completed the forms given to me by the receptionist, who had no interest in the tears running down my face or the snot that was forming a miniature puddle at the top of my lip. She made no eye contact, offered no consolation, and spoke fast and monotone as if she were a robot providing basic-skills directions to a dumb human who expected humanity from a metal machine.

It took longer than it should have to complete the paperwork. My hand seemed to be in direct communication with my heart, and my heart was sending the message, "Don't do this." Other patients entering the office also distracted me, as I was hoping, in vain, that one of the faces would belong to him. Finally, I handed the completed documents to Rachel the Robot and stood there like a dummy waiting for her to say something or give me some signal as to what to do next. She looked up to find me standing there, and with a "these humans are so stupid" tone, muttered, "Sit down, the nurse will call you when they're ready."

I took a seat as far from the alien as possible. I tried passing the time by fingering through a magazine, but the sight of bald babies and smiling mothers nauseated me. Why the hell would anyone put family magazines in the waiting area of an abortion clinic? I went to the bathroom, although I didn't need to use it. Made a pit stop by the water fountain, bent down to take a sip, and remembered the pre-op instructions, "No food or drink after mid-night." Left with nothing else to do, I folded. Cupped my face in my hands and let it out. I heard a door open and close; with hesitant faith and no desire to meet the pathetic eyes of yet another stranger, I refrained from investigating the new entry into the clinic.

"Come on, let's go."

I looked up to find him standing over me.

"What did you say?"

"I said, we're leaving. Look, Trina, I know we're young and neither of us knows the first thing about raising a baby ... but umm ... we can't do this. I don't know if we'll be together forever ... I mean ... I hope we'll be together forever. Either way, *I'm* not killing my son."

Another alien was in my midst. I was surrounded.

This one must be malfunctioning because he was actually displaying human-like feelings. I wondered whether his leaders would allow him to remain on earth with the glitch or whether they would come retrieve him late in the dark of night and return him to Mars where they would replace the emotions chip, which some idiot had mistakenly placed in him, with the same gadgets Robot Rachel had installed behind her breastplate. I stared at him a while, unsure of what to make of it. He reached out his hand; I held it and stood up. I passed RR on the way out and reported, "I'm keeping the baby."

No reply. Just gave me one final, "dumb humans" glare.

The remainder of my freshman year was bleak. Morning sickness – afternoon sickness – night sickness; I finished my first year with a cumulative average of 0.6 and left school on academic probation. Daddy hadn't spoken to me from the time I had made my announcement. And upon meeting my unborn child's other set of grandparents, I was introduced to a new meaning of feeling like a piece of shit. They were refined and polished and spoke to me using small words, as if larger words would clog and shut down my brain cells. To them, I was the girl from Newark, New Jersey, with the countrified, backward ass parents. We were all diabolically working in cahoots to trap their son into some back-alley deal that would ruin their family's good name among the black bourgeois, have their vacationing rights at Martha's Vineyard revoked, and pilfer all of the diligence and industry they had endured to separate themselves from the average, indolent hood negroes.

There were many things I would have liked to say to them. "Kiss my and my parents' asses," topped the list; instead, in their company I said very little. They were different black people than the ones I was accustomed to; in their presence I was out of my element.

Every time I stepped into their Riverside, luxury condo, it seemed I had fumbled my way onto the set of the taping of an episode of *The Cosby Show*. I, being the girl Theo bought home from college, knocked up, in the season finale. They, praying that the writers would have sense enough to open the new season with an episode in which Theo finds out the girl isn't really pregnant by him. Then he and Cliff share a moving moment at the conclusion of the half-hour, as Theo emotionally declares (with Cliff's arm lovingly draped over his shoulder) that he has learned his lesson and promises to be more responsible. Not exactly how the real-life version worked out.

Although in some strange way I admired the Huxtables, my mother felt quite differently. Mother tolerated them, but refused to put on airs to present herself as something that she wasn't. So when Clair decided to advise my mother that "it would be best for Katrina and the child if she finishes her studies part-time at a local school," my mother advised her of a few things that I'm sure Bill Cosby would have never allowed to be written into the script of his show.

Daddy sat back and watched the buffoonery from a distance, showing no interest in the petty bickering or my idiotic desire to be accepted by the Huxtables. We never spoke of it, but I presume he was more distressed about my future than anything else. So, Daddy was not a visitor, bearing balloons and flowers, during my maternity ward stay. During the first week after I returned home, he continued the silent treatment, ignoring both his new grandson and me. As Fate would have it, Daddy's silence was forever broken the following Sunday and he fell in love with his little man.

That day was rough – damn rough. I watched the blue compact car exiting the driveway, filled to capacity, with all the necessities of campus living. The driver promised he would call as soon as he arrived at school. Although I smiled at this statement in his sight, the smile was replaced with tears as soon as the car disappeared around the corner.

The here and now of the crying baby and the diapers and formula-making and 3:00 AM feedings were more than my twenty-year old mind wanted to embrace. It wasn't cute anymore. And the creatively wallpapered Mickey-Mouse-themed room with the lovely crib and changing table and rocker and dresser teeming with Gymboree and Baby Gap outfits, would have been traded in a split second for a dorm room with a twin bed, 26-inch TV, books, professors, frat parties, and an opportunity to get the hell out of this God-forsaken place.

I understood the hurt in Daddy's face now. His fear, in a matter of moments, had become my own. Single, black, female – someone's mother. Now what? I sat on the front porch for a long while. It was August and hot. I listened, indifferently, to the cacophony of staccato resonances that played in my neighborhood: music blaring; sirens; kids yelling as they played in the street; and people passing by engaged in a myriad of incomprehensible conversations.

I thought back to the nineteen-year-old, who left with no other means of transportation for a weekend home, set out on her first expedition from Philadelphia's Thirtieth Street Train Station to Newark's Penn Station. And while on the bus, completing the last leg of the journey home, she had come to a new awareness of the city that she had always been proud to claim. It was different now; something had changed. There was more garbage. There were more lost and desperate-looking people on the corners. There were more liquor stores and more abandoned apartment buildings. There were more black boys face-down on the ground with the boot heals of officers in their backs. There were more girls pushing strollers while holding the hand of a toddler and toting baby number three in belly. Observing this, the nineteen-year-old had decided then and there, that she would make something of herself and come back to help heal her dying community.

But she had gotten caught up with a boy and sidetracked by the awe of a first real romance. And a year later she found herself sitting on the stoop, reflections abruptly halted by the screams of the crying baby who needed his pamper changed or formula made or a nap or something else that she wasn't prepared to give.

She walked into the house, passing her father, who was pre-occupied with the Mets, Dodgers, and a Miller, entered her bedroom and placed the wailing baby down in the bassinet. She proceeded to lie in bed and made a futile attempt to obstruct the annoyance of the infant's imploring bellows by placing the pillow over her head. The father, perhaps during a commercial break, heard the calamity and came to investigate. He demanded that the girl get up and tend to her child. The girl did not stir. Her father sensed that his commands would remain unheeded and picked up the child and carried him off.

Worried, the girl got up after some time and went to check on her child and father. She found them both asleep in front of the television. She joined them and rested her head on her dad's shoulder. She cried so hard her body was shaking – partly from shame – partly from the sight of her dad holding the baby – and partly from a weight that was mysteriously released. Her father urged her to stop crying, promising that all would work itself out.

Ironic, it's been all these years later, and it's still difficult to relay that story unless it is told in the third person.

Daddy was right though; things did work themselves out. I learned how to be a mommy. The next spring I went back to school far more focused; I was responsible for someone else other than myself now. In fact, I received special permission to exceed the semester credit maximum and took extra classes each semester and at least two classes each summer. I graduated with the class I had come in with. My determination was spurred on by Mrs. Huxtable's remark, "What's the point of her going back? She's too far behind to catch up."

I went back and I caught up. I recall crossing the stage to receive my degree, looking out into the audience and spotting the most magnificent little boy up on a man's shoulders. It dawned on me that he was my baby (now three years old) on my daddy's shoulders. And I was as proud of them as they were of me.

Over the course of the next fourteen years, I believe I did more things that made Daddy proud than not. I became an English teacher, a department team leader, a vice principal, earned a master's degree, and was overall (in my estimation) a pretty good person, mother, and daughter. I did marry a man that Daddy did not care for – the first husband. His flashy clothes and cars did not impress Daddy, nor did his charisma. Daddy called him The Con Artist.

I was twenty-six, with two children (the second of which was created with The Con Artist) and a second-year teacher. Mother, being fond of flash and charisma, thought it was simply wonderful when he showed up with a ring and a proposal. I wasn't so sure. But I took the trip to Vegas, got drunk as hell, and laughed the entire time as the odd-looking man performed the nuptials in the little, white chapel on the strip. I wore a red dress – can you imagine – a red dress? It was symbolic of our two-year marriage: hot like fire. We fucked and fought - fought and fucked; it was the Two-F relationship. I was feisty, my attitude was awful, I had a very short fuse, and no tolerance or patience for nonsense. He was handsome and slick; he liked the ladies and the ladies liked him. He and I made a cute couple, yet we were never truly a married couple. Once the speculation of his cheating had been transformed into official evidence, I joined in and invited a new boyfriend to the party.

It gets tiring sooner or later, though. The sneaking, the lying, and the remembering to make sure your girlfriend is aware that she and you were together last weekend.

I woke up one day and decided that I didn't want to be married anymore. It wasn't just the indiscretions; as I've admitted, we were both guilty of that. It was really about the manner in which he allowed his mother to treat our child. She didn't like me and she took that out on my baby. She would do silly shit like send a Christmas present for the Con Artist's son, from a previous relationship, and give nothing to our daughter. That was cool, because I would do lap dances in the middle of Times Square before my daughter would ever need anything from her, but I couldn't respect a man who would allow anyone to mistreat his child.

In addition, The Con Artist went to great lengths to smash my aspirations. I would mention going back to school and he would come up with fifty reasons why I shouldn't. I've done a number of foolish things with men but dealing with a destroyer of dreams isn't one of them. Shortly after our daughter's second birthday, I had moved out and into my own apartment. Eighteen months later

> **A Few Words About When a Woman Cheats**
> **One**: *You will not catch her unless she chooses to be caught.*
>
> **Two**: *If and when she chooses to have her game detected, better believe the purpose is to hurt the man worse than he has hurt her (even for the worst womanizer, it is hard to imagine his woman with her ass in the air and he not be the dude behind her.)*
>
> **Three**: *Unlike men, (most) women cheat with a man who is formidable enough to replace the husband/boyfriend if necessary.*
>
> **Four**: *It is not woman's ego that is fed by cheating, it usually a need to fill a void and/or her thirst for revenge.*

the divorce was final based on Irreconcilable Differences, which in laymen's terms means it's best to allow these jokers to get as far away from each other as possible before someone is in need of medical attention, bail, or both.

Chapter Five

I fell in love for the first time in September of 1999. His longtime friend and my college roommate were tying the knot; he was a groomsmen and I a bridesmaid. I was drawn to him from the moment I saw him. He was a beautiful brown with beautiful locks and a beautiful face. He made everyone laugh and enjoy the tedious wedding rehearsal. I was eager to see him again on the day of the wedding.

He appeared in his tux, hair put up, goatee freshly groomed. It was definitely hard to focus on anything other than him. At the reception, I went over to the table where my parents were accompanied by another couple, pointed Mr. Fine out and announced that I had every intention of making him my man. The gentleman who was seated with his wife, across the table from my parents, smirked and said, "I'm sure he'll be happy about that."

I responded, "Do you know him?"

And he followed with, "I've known him for twenty-eight years. That's my son!"

That story still makes me smile. My father-in-law enjoyed telling it too while showing the first picture he took of us shortly after I embarrassed myself in front of the parents of the man I intended to make mine. And oh, how we danced that evening. Two years later we had a child and a home. Two years after that we danced all night at our own wedding.

It didn't last very long. It only took three years for me to sabotage our marriage. I won't accept all the blame though; it was a combination of both our faults.

He was and still is an excellent father to all three children. He was a provider and protector – and he supported my endeavors. He just wasn't ready to be married. I pushed my desire to be married. And because he loved me, he folded and gave me what I wanted. In heated arguments, I would accuse him of marrying me only because of our daughter; I knew that wasn't true. I suppose, in afterthought, it was too much for him. The carefree bachelor turned husband, father of three, guard and co-breadwinner of the

> *Getting him isn't the hard part. Keeping him is the part that requires work.*

home. And in all of it, he fought tenaciously to retain his freedom.

In my thinking, freedom was sacrificed in exchange for "I do." I realize now that that line of reasoning is illogical and will certainly contribute to the detriment of a relationship. I expected the fun-loving, free spirit to surrender his life for his new family. Although it is necessary to enter into and remain in a marriage with the understanding that the playa card has expired, I don't believe it is equally necessary to give up who you are. I wish I had known that then.

I wish I had been cool with him going out to have a few with the fellas. I wish I had understood the significance of allowing him his space and his need to be treated and trusted as a man – instead of as my fourth child who was constantly interrogated and made to answer for his every movement. I wish I had loved myself enough not to be so insecure and jealous. But wish as I might, that damage was done long ago and some things that are broken cannot be fixed. Although we get along well and are great co-parents now, there was a time when we loathed each other. There was a period when the sight of him made me physically sick, and I'm certain he felt the same reaction upon seeing me.

Things began pretty well, as most relationships do. But then the arguing, and the accusing, and the belittling, and the disrespecting started. He swears he never cheated, but the run-ins I had with other women proved otherwise. When we reached the point of physical fighting, I knew our days were numbered; my father had never lifted a hand to me and I'd be damned if I was going to allow another man to do so. A push, a grab, a mush led to police reports of domestic violence and court appearances. And our children watched it all.

I remember arguing with him about something (which could have been about anything, because by year two we debated everything). I clearly recall him standing at the bottom of the stairs and me standing at the top, and both of us yelling and cursing at each other. The melee ended with me being dragged down the stairs and kicked in the back while on the floor. He left, slamming the door as a final gesture of his anger, and I looked back to see my three- and eight-year old daughters staring down at me. I didn't say a word. As if everything was fine, I got up from the floor and proceeded to get the girls and myself prepared to leave.

The three of us drove the hour to my graduate class in silence. Once we arrived, I set them up in the lobby area near the classroom with their snacks and books. They both examined me closely the entire time. I realized I should have used the hour drive to explain that hitting is wrong, that they should never allow anyone to hit them, nor should they ever hit anyone else. But I didn't; I was too ashamed and embarrassed to even make eye contact with them; I couldn't get the words out to have a conversation.

During our lunch break, my professor saw me sitting with my daughters and came over to meet them. As he was standing next to the table speaking, my younger daughter got out of her chair, walked up to him, and kicked him in the leg. I was mortified. He laughed it off, said a few more things, and walked away. My daughter had resumed coloring as if nothing happened. At first I was at a loss for words. When I finally asked, "Why did you kick that man?"

Her reply was, "Daddy did it to you, Mommy." Needless to say, I didn't return to class after lunch. Twenty minutes into the drive home, I attempted to begin my speech about violence, but the girls had already fallen asleep. During the remainder of the trip, I thought about the disconnect between the things I was trying to teach my children and what they were actually learning from me. And I prayed that my husband and I could salvage our marriage and be the role models that our children needed. But by the end, he and I hadn't accomplished either of those things.

Our last year together in the house was similar to the movie *War of the Roses*. I had threatened to take my wedding ring off the next time he stated what had become his favorite line, "I'm not your son. Do not ask me where I'm going or when I'll be back."

The next time he said it, I took the rings off. Three months later, New Year's Eve 2005, he stayed out all night for the first time. He managed to make an appearance, tired and disheveled, in time for breakfast. The children were seated at the table waiting for me to finish buttering the toast; he walked into the kitchen, and I immediately began with the verbal assault.

"You must be out of your fucking mind if you think I'm the woman who's going to tolerate this bullshit!" (In between sipping champagne and watching the ball drop I had practiced that opening line for hours).

He responded with two words: "Shut up."

Now this is a no-no. A woman is clearly pissed, emotional, and has stayed up all night wondering what funky trick you had your funky penis in; and how you could possibly have the audacity to stay out all night, but to do it on a New Year's Eve makes it so much worse; and you have the balls to say "shut up" ... Huh?

I was prepared to say so many things. I had planned to start by saying that I was trying to be a good wife, but it seemed that all I received in return for my effort was criticism. Then I intended to ask why did he get married if he still wanted to chase women and run the street all the time? And I figured I would close with helping him understand that if he couldn't love me back, the right way, he could just take his raggedy ass back where he had just come from. But in the words of Robert Burns, "The best laid plans of mice and men often go awry." Mine sure as hell did that day.

Maybe he knew what I would say; I'm sure I had said most of it a countless number of times before. So he had a speech of his own prepared – just two words: "Shut Up." When he said it, his voice didn't rise nor did he become animated. He simply stated the words, "shut up" as would a man who was tired of being someone's husband and ready to scratch his name off as the cosigner on the marriage certificate.

As he sat at the kitchen table and began placing food on his plate, he said nothing else. I was enraged. Our story may have turned out much differently if I had let him have his breakfast and waited to address the situation at a later time when we were both prepared to discuss it. Or maybe waiting for a better place and time would have done little to save our marriage; I'll never know. In that moment I was infuriated. My heart was wounded; my pride and ego were wounded; and to top it off, he had destroyed my well-thought-out plan with just two words: *shut* and *up*.

I punched him in his mouth as hard as I could. I had never hit him before. And I knew I would only have the opportunity to get one hit, so I tried to make it one that counted. What followed was food and dishes flying – kids screaming, crying and ducking – and two people who were previously very much in love, saying and doing all manners of evil, which are usually reserved for bitter enemies. The only good that came from this incident was that he never laid his hands on me again.

I contacted the realtor the next day; the *For Sale* sign was on the front lawn the following afternoon. If hell exists, I am certain it is a place similar to the culture of the house we lived in during the following eight months while we attempted to sell it. Neither of us had any intention of leaving the house before it sold; in some deranged way that would be admitting defeat to the other. We both stayed. Sleeping in separate bedrooms – existing as estranged roommates who did everything possible to persuade the other to move out.

It was war, and I was a bitch on the battlefield. I was a woman scorned and my arsenal was indicative of such. I would cook and make just enough for the kids and I to eat. Washing his clothes or doing any other chore that benefited him was out of the question. I started having an affair and would have phone conversations with my friend right in front of him; he did the same. Once our affairs were out in the open, we would attempt to beat the other at leaving the house. The winner was awarded the honor of spending the evening out; second-place prize was staying home with the children.

Our behavior was nonsensical. But hurt people, hurt people. And we were both hurting quite badly. By the time there was a buyer for the house, we had crossed the lines of respect and obliterated any possible chance of reconciliation. On the last day, his moving truck transported him and his belongings back to his hometown. Mine took three children, a number of boxes and bags, and me across town to a townhome complex.

Of all the tomfoolery that occurred during those eight months, the regret that I will always carry with me is the way I behaved when my father-in-law passed. He was the first man I had ever met who measured up to my dad. I loved Pop-Pop dearly, not just because he didn't judge me or because he was so kind to my children, but because he was one of those rare human beings who deposited far more than he withdrew from the lives of others. He died two weeks after that New Year's Day.

Even though it was a bitterly painful loss for me and far more so for my husband, I mourned apart from him. I was physically present at the funeral services but I did not grieve with him. My support and encouragement were no longer things I had to give. So when he suggested that maybe we should put off selling the house, his words fell on deaf ears. And when I'd find him sitting, sobbing in the dark, I refused to allow myself to offer comfort. And as soon as the funeral home limousines returned from the gravesite and parked in front of the church, I thanked the driver for assisting me out and headed for my car instead of joining his family for the repast. I wasn't a member of his clan any longer, and this was more devastating than all else.

As much as we sometimes desire that they don't, relationships extend past two people, to others (family, friends, and foes), who are intertwined, for better or worse, in the union. The reversal of vows often ends not only the connection with a mate, but with all others who were connected to the mate as well. You tell your story, he tells his, and everyone picks a side. Even if anyone is sympathetic to the other side's rendition of events, it's usually most pragmatic to remain loyal to the home team. He and his relatives were no longer my family, and the reality of this chiseled away yet another piece of me that has yet to be replaced.

Chapter Six

Combat officially concluded in August of 2006. Having been so consumed with my life, I had not seen much of my parents for a good while. The next time I saw my dad he was noticeably thinner. His responses to my questions about his health were that he was having some stomach pains here and there but the doctors had run every test and all was well. Over the next several months, Daddy's strong, bulky build reduced to half of its once robust frame.

In February of the following year, Daddy went to the emergency room early one morning, complaining of severe stomach discomfort. By the time I got off work that afternoon, situated the kids, and drove the hour to Newark, he was still waiting to be examined and had spent the last ten hours on a stretcher in the ER hallway.

I showed my whole ass! I promised to have Johnny Cochrane and the entire damn Dream Team there if someone with a medical degree didn't attend to my dad in the next hour. I called his private physician and promised that if she didn't come to that hospital I would drive to her office and drag her there myself. I carried on like a lunatic. But it was my daddy, and in thirty-seven years I had not once seen him in pain or suffering. I would have happily gone to jail that night or been admitted to a rubber room if it meant my father would receive the treatment he needed.

A few days later, Daddy was diagnosed with stage four-pancreatic cancer. The doctors informed him that it was irreversible and that because of his age and condition he was not a candidate for surgery. What I said in reply to this was "screw the doctors!" I spent the next two months fighting for my dad's life. I researched, I contacted specialists, I argued with physicians and nurses and everyone else who provided care for my dad – and I endlessly debated my mother on the best course of action. I never slept. I rarely ate. My son, then seventeen, took on many of the charges of our home including: cooking, making sure his sisters ate, did their homework, bathed, and behaved. I was unavailable mentally, physically, emotionally – unavailable.

A world without Daddy was inconceivable. Who would ever love me the way he did again? I needed him to stay. I could fix it, like he had fixed things a countless number of times for me. Whatever the cost, whatever the sacrifice, whatever I was required to do; I had resolved that Daddy was not leaving me. I promised God that if He would allow him to stay, I would be eternally grateful and forever indebted to Him. But I guess God knew something that I refused to acknowledge: the course of Daddy's journey was complete; he had labored and he had loved, he had laughed and he had lived – and now it was his time to hear God say, "Job well done," receive his wings, and rest.

When the doctor confirmed that he would release Daddy into home hospice care or a nursing home, the volcano that existed between my mother and me began to erupt. Daddy said he wished to spend his last days in his home. My mother argued that although the nurse would come two hours each day, the remaining care would be in her hands, and she was unable and unwilling to do it alone.

I was furious. If my father was to be admitted to a nursing home, it would be over my cold, dead body. I didn't care if I had to quit my job and move home; he had earned the right to return to his bed, in his room, in his house – and that's where he was going. There were a few "selfish-bitches" and "fuck yous" thrown around between my mother and me for several days before it dissolved into silence. Each of us, more alike than we would ever confess, had no intention of allowing the other to have her way. In the end, neither of us won the conflict. Daddy's condition worsened; he could no longer speak or swallow. He was moved to the terminal cancer floor of the hospital and remained there until his death.

It was Friday evening and the beginning of spring break. As I entered Daddy's hospital room, my mother was putting on her coat. We said nothing. I tried not to look at her, but I couldn't help but notice how slow she was moving and the exhaustion in her face. It never occurred to me that she was losing someone too, and that it was draining her as well. She kissed Daddy on the cheek and left. I positioned the chair, my mother had occupied, closer to the bed. I started talking, as if we were engaged in a mutual conversation. Daddy nodded here and there, and attempted to smile a few times. The last thing I told him was that he was the best man I had ever known. He shook his head in agreement, and then fell asleep shortly after. I held his hand and listened to Donnie Hathaway's "A Song for You," over and over again.

Chapter Six

It was April 14, 2007. Morning came, my eyes, on instinct, went to the heart monitor – "still among the living," I happily commented to myself. I rose and stretched to regain the feeling in my cramped body. I examined Daddy; he appeared calm. Satisfied with this, I decided to go down to the cafeteria and grab some breakfast. Upon my return, a short time later, I found Daddy awake and gazing in my direction. "Hey, handsome, I ..."

He took three deep breaths and was still. I'm not sure why I looked at the clock; it was 9:00 AM. The heart monitor began to make a buzzing noise; I found no reason to give it or the nurse it signaled my attention. I sat back down in the chair and held Daddy's hand. Another nurse and then a doctor came in; they worked around me. I did not move until one of them reached to close his eyes; I said I would do it and did. I suppose one of the nurses called my mother. She and my brother arrived and we all just sat there, realizing the tie that bound us together had just been broken. It was a dull pain at first, which was agitated and made more pronounced when the nurse asked, "Is it okay to cover him now?" Mother shook her head "Yes." I felt differently but chose not to impose my will on the matter.

I had witnessed Daddy taking his last breath. I was in shock. Unable to cry or speak or to fathom the depth of what was going on, I was a silent observer, as everyone and everything around me seemed to move in extremely slow motion.

It wasn't until we were at the house and my mother requested her nephews to come over and help her go through my father's documents that it hit me that I was left unprotected in the world. She was in charge now. My father's body was still warm, but this didn't stop her from showing out.

Confused, I asked, "Would you like me to do anything?"

She directed me to dust the furniture, as "There will be people coming here."

Did she instruct me to dust while she and her nephews go through MY daddy's things? It was enough that she refused my attempt to hug her in the hospital; now I was being sent to do housework. I found my brother on the porch. He took little interest in what had just occurred between Mother and me, other than to say, "What did you expect?"

One of her nephews appeared outside after gently informing mother that he was uncomfortable with her request and believed that it was a task that my brother and I should be handling. I thought that was decent of him, but her wrath had just begun.

Later that night, I attempted to intercede in a discussion of the plans for the funeral. She stated, and I quote, "Stay out of it; you're the adopted daughter!"

The statement engulfed my entire being with a rage that no words can describe. I had never raised my hand to my mother, nor do I condone such behavior, yet she had made it perfectly clear that I was now no one's daughter; she invited the ass whipping that was about to commence. What saved her, or me, or both, was the first set of hands that restrained me before I could reach the other side of the kitchen. It took every adult in the house to carry me out. In the midst of the pandemonium, I heard her scream, "Don't ever come back here, bitch! Don't you ever step foot inside my house again!" For a considerable amount of time, I abided by those commands.

Daddy's funeral drew scores of mourners; both those who offered private and public condolences expressed truly deeply-felt sentiments. In the midst of consoling my children and brother, I sat there thinking that this was the kind of farewell indicative of one who had led a good life. I pray the farewell to my existence on this Earth will afford me such.

At the cemetery, I refused to unite with those who congregated in a semi-circular fashion to hear the pastor render his final remarks and place the single red or white rose on the sky-bluish casket. Alone, I viewed the last service from a distance; this formality was too final and personal a procedure for me to participate in. Daddy and I would reunite again, until then he would exist in my spirit. And he would survive in the way someone would tell a story or a joke, or would do something or say something in a manner akin to his. And I would remember him while reminiscing with my children or my brother about our fallen hero. And when there was no one else who could understand this hurt, I would confide in him.

Perhaps because I spent most of it drunk, I have no recollection of the year that followed. I never truly understood substance abuse until then. A consistent intoxicated state seemed to lessen the cutting pain of remembering. I chose, at that time, to forget. There were so very many things I wanted to forget: the last three breaths, the woman who disowned me, the husband who hated me, and the necessity of returning to Earth to resume being a mommy.

Chapter Six

Sometime later, when the juncture on my journey led my path to cross Coach, I was fragile and severely damaged. I was in dire need of someone to rescue me from myself. I thought it was him who would save me – The Man in the Blue Suit. In retrospect, I understand that hoping for someone to *save you* is an unrealistic expectation that one should refrain from positioning upon another. I presume that I sought a replacement for daddy. But it is asinine to expect a love interest to play proxy for a parent; they are two entirely different roles.

Yet, I was determined to replace what I had lost. So, I gave a concerted effort to strong-arm Coach into a space that he was not created to occupy. My neediness to be held, to be cared for, to be loved – resulted in his scathing contempt for my antics and a retreat from me to those who conducted themselves more sensibly.

And now, a year after the blood – a year after the hamster's tired legs gave way – a year after that which had been closest to my heart had become the farthest removed – he stood behind me, awaiting confirmation that I, in fact, was Grasshopper. I, being uncertain as to the response of this query, hesitated to reply.

Book Two

Twelve Days

(Otherwise Entitled: A Few Things I Needed to Say on the Day of Mother's Funeral)

My mother was a courageous woman.

When it was not fashionable but was considered taboo my mother found two abandoned babies and made them her own.

Even as the ignorant folk attempted in vain to persuade her to believe that she was less than a woman because she could not bear children from her womb,

She held her head up – held the tears back – rendered voiceless the pain of the hurtful criticism – and ascended to the epitome of womanhood, by giving life, not from her womb, but from her heart.

My mother and I did not share the same blood, the

same ancestry, or the same lineage – and yet, she was my mother, and I was her child.

As a daughter, a mother, and an educator for the past sixteen years, I have often asked myself the question: What is it that constitutes a parent-child relationship?

Some suggest that it is the sharing of DNA.

But there are people who are the spitting image of each other – yet they commit all manners of evil against one another.

So perhaps the sharing of DNA is not a pre-requisite for a parent-child relationship.

Maybe then, a parent-child relationship lies in the ability of two people to always get along.

I unequivocally disagree.

My mother and I were like oil and water; we fought like cats and dogs.

And yet, there was never a time when one needed the other that the other was not right there.

This leads me to the conclusion then, that it is quite possible, that the success of a parent-child relationship lies in the willingness to open one's heart enough to selflessly remain ever present by another's side.

My mother came to my home for the last twelve days of her life – and we remained by each other's sides.

In those twelve days we found redemption.

In those twelve days we found forgiveness.

In those twelve days we found the true meaning of love.

Because in those twelve days, together, we found God.

So you see, the last twelve days of her living on this earth were the first twelve of mine.

And so, I no longer question the meaning of a parent-child relationship.

Thank God,

Now, I know.

Chapter Seven

I was five years old. The offspring of my mother's thirteen brothers and sisters, along with my brother and I, had received implicit directives to form a line, assembled in size order, to receive a coin from my maternal grandmother. I, being the youngest and smallest in height, found myself at the end of the gift line. It was a long line. I stood, for what seemed like hours, watching as each of the cousins made their way to The Grandmother, observing how she happily reached into her old, battered change purse, withdrew a shiny token of affection, and embraced the receiver, as he or she lovingly returned her hugs and kisses – as grandparents and grandchildren do.

I was so excited that it was hard to contain myself. The Grandmother was actually going to hug and kiss me; this was big! This was Jackson Five, Soul Train, Wonder Woman, Barbie Doll House, Getting My Hair Pressed for Kindergarten Pictures, Having the Most Lines in the Easter, Christmas, and Vacation Bible School Plays (cause I could read before I could walk, which is what daddy said). Big! The coin, itself, was of no consequence to me. I could've cared less about the money side of the impending transaction; I just wanted the hug and kiss from The Grandmother who really never spoke to me, or was kind to me, or took any interest in having me sit on her lap and play fondly (as I had seen her do with the cousins).

Ours was a relationship of fear: I feared the way she looked down at me; I feared the day when she would make good on her promise to "tear my ass out the socket" if I didn't "get somewhere and sit" my "half-breed, piss-colored ass down"; and I feared most that I really was the "bad-ass little bastard" that she said I was. So I tried really hard to be a good-girl – especially around The Grandmother. I stood, at-attention, solider-still, on that line – my little body erect, arms and hands straight as a board, as if someone had crazy-glued them to the yellow sundress I had been forced to wear for our journey to the South.

"Your grandmother loves yellow," said Mom, as she had taken the polyester, sunshine bright, configuration of flowers, lace, and bows out of the shopping bag. Of course, I put the foolish thing on. Number One: it's not like I had a choice in the matter; I'm sure my mother was speaking more to herself than to my resistance about wearing the awful thing. Or perhaps, she was contemplating out loud as to how she could make me more appealing to her mother. Number Two: I wanted to please The Grandmother.

I knew she didn't like me. I believe it ironic that adults often think that kids don't have a clue as to what is going on around them. Kids know far more than we give them credit for knowing. Even when the grown-ups, in all their infinite wisdom, decide to converse, using big words and/or spelling out the bad words, a child can sense and make sense of the happenings going on around her. In my case, I could sense that I was somehow different from my brother and the cousins; I just really didn't know how or why. In any case, it made sense (to me) that to avoid "getting my ass torn out the socket" it would be best to give The Grandmother what she wanted. Dumb yellow dress it was.

My brother was in front of me on line. He and The Grandmother were okay. I mean, she wasn't doing flips when she saw him coming, but she was far more congenial with him than she was with me. Their exchange was brief. With the cousins, I watched her make silly faces as she toyed with the contents of the change purse, before extracting what one would have believed was a solid gold nugget and placing it in the cousin's hand. Then she kissed the hand and the face of the new owner of the coin, which was followed by laughter and tight grandma squeezes. With my brother, the exchange was more formal; like a business transaction between two semi-well acquainted associates. After my brother stepped up to greet her, she took out a quarter, handed it to him, hugged him quickly, as if he might be carrying some transmittable disease that she would surely catch from prolonged contact, and their exchange was complete.

My turn! The Grandmother, momentarily, glanced me over. I hoped she would compliment my yellow dress; she did not. Instead, over exaggerating her movements, she closed the change purse, laid it on the brown-stained wooden lamp table and motioned for one of her sons to come and assist her out of the rocker she had occupied. I frantically looked around The Grandmother's parlor, searching the faces to locate one that showed a trace of sympathy for this tragedy.

The cousins, the aunts, the uncles, and other nameless kinfolk, absorbed in their own playing and fighting and drinking and small talk and gossip, were purposely ignorant of my demise. I did not see Daddy,

Chapter Seven

or Mom, or Brother; and left alone to fend for myself, I did what most five-year-olds would do in that situation: I cried. You know that scream-cry that children are apt to do after falling off a bike, or being lost in the mall, or being disappointed by the refusal of a parent to buy the action figure of their favorite cartoon character, or when realizing that the people who are supposed to protect, and love, and nurture you are full of crap – and it is beyond your control to make them stop acting so stupid? I balled my little fists, closed my eyes, and scream-cried long after Daddy heard me and hauled me out to the porch.

"See what I mean? Taking on some other whore's throw-away ain't nothin' but trouble. Lil' hussy got all kinds of emotional problems."

This, The Grandmother announced (to anyone who was listening) as Daddy and I made our way through the raggedy screen door. At some point I fell asleep. Who knows how long I cried – maybe until I thought it was all out, but it was never all out.

During my second of two encounters with a therapist, I recalled this childhood event. At the end of the session, the therapist suggested that I draft a letter to The Grandmother, telling her how her treatment had made me feel and how it had affected me. Walking to my car, I questioned why the hell I was paying someone one hundred and seventy-five bucks an hour, to advise me to write a letter to someone who had been dead for over thirty years. But I figured she was the professional, so maybe she knew what she was talking about. I got home, poured myself a glass of wine, and sat staring at the blank, yellow page of the legal pad.

I had had no direct contact with The Grandmother after the "Coins for Hugs Affair"; Daddy made sure of that. The remainder of that visit, some three decades ago, was spent under his close supervision. Finally, when it was time to say our good-byes, Daddy instructed me to remain in the rental car.

"You want to teach the girl to be ill-mannered, Johnny?" I could hear my mother question as my parents and brother walked toward The Grandmother's house. After reaching a significant distance from the car, Daddy and Mom stopped walking (sending my brother ahead) and Daddy was talking. I couldn't hear what was said, but I could tell from the side view of his face that Daddy was pissed. I didn't see Mom offer any rebuttal to Daddy's words. After a few moments, they went inside the house.

I was glad that I didn't have to say goodbye to The Grandmother. If I were older, I would have wondered

Chapter Seven

what they were saying and whether Mom had to offer an excuse for my absence from the farewell ceremony. But again, I was five. I did what five-year-olds do: play with my Barbie, Ken, Baby Barbie, Baby Ken, and the fluffy, brown BarbieKenBabies's dog and imagined that they were all hugging and kissing and loving each other like families do.

Some time later, my imagination was cut short by the opening of the front car door, followed by its being slammed shut. It was Daddy. He mumbled something to himself – I think some words I wasn't allowed to say. Then he scanned the backseat (via the front rearview mirror) until he located me staring into his reflection. Straining to smile, he asked, "How's my baby girl doing?"

I replied that I was fine or something close to it, so that Daddy wouldn't have to fight so hard to smile. But Daddy was no longer eying me; his focus had now transitioned toward the house. I scooted up to my knees to catch a peek at what held his attention. I saw Mom, Brother, and The Grandmother on the front porch. The Grandmother was patting my brother on the head; Mother was smiling.

"Patting him on his head like a damn dog ... a damn dog ... and this fool is smiling ..." the words bitterly came from the driver's seat. I thought to tell Daddy that Brother isn't a dog – he's a boy – but I didn't get the feeling that that comment would be welcome. But if The Grandmother did believe that Brother was a dog, I guess that was okay, because people love dogs. Maybe she thought I was a cockroach; no one wants to pet, or hold, or play with a cockroach.

I didn't see The Grandmother again until her funeral. I was seven then, a big-little girl. It was the first funeral that I had ever attended and I had lots of questions: 1) Why does everyone have on black? 2) Are people crying because they're sad she's dead or because they're happy she's not alive anymore? 3) Is the preacher paid to say nice things about a dead person, even if the person wasn't nice? And 4) Does God let people who were mean to children come to Heaven?

I knew there was no chance of having these concerns rectified by any adult, so I kept them to myself until I asked my brother later. His response to all of my inquiries: I don't know – I don't know – Probably – Probably not. For apparent reasons, I was not satisfied with his answers, but in the absence of any other trusting soul to confide in, I dismissed my queries as my brother had.

Now, thirty-two years later, I held on to those

Chapter Seven

questions and many others as I attempted to write a letter to a woman who had recklessly destroyed some part of my innocence and my heart a very long time ago.

I'm not sure whether it was the third glass of chardonnay that helped to ease the words from my spirit, but without warning, the dam was overflowing; there was no way to stop it now.

> *Dear Grandmother,*
>
> *(Let's be clear from the door, I am only addressing you as Grandmother for three reasons: because I've been taught to respect my elders; for lack of a better term of endearment; and because I figure that starting by saying "Dear Bitch" would sound just a little more hostile than I'd like to).*
>
> *Anyway, there are few things that I would like to say to you. I've held these things in for quite some time, and I know that not having expressed them has somehow negatively affected me. The first thing I need to say is that you had no right to treat a child the way you treated me. Why would you do that? Why would anyone do that? What did I do to you that made you hate me?*
>
> *It's funny, I can't remember some things from*

last week – but I clearly recall the day that I wore that yellow dress to impress you (because Mother said it was your favorite color), and I waited in line to hug and kiss you, but when you got to me, you closed your change purse and walked away.

I didn't want your money, nor have I ever needed your money. Daddy has made damn sure I never needed a coin from you or anyone else. I just wanted to be your granddaughter – that's all. But you wouldn't let me. The absolute worst part of all of this is that you rubbed off on my mom. Instead of supporting your daughter through difficult situations, you made her feel like a piece of shit for not being able to have children.

And the light-skin/dark-skin country, ignorant bullshit that you put in her head caused me to have many sad days of hearing your venom in her voice as she called me "half-breed" and "piss-color." My relationship with my mother has always been fucked up because you were fucked up – and you fucked her up.

I would like to slap the shit out of you just one good time. Or maybe "beat your ass out of *the socket" the way you promised you would do to me for doing things like trying to read a book to you, or showing you my church awards or just sitting and minding my damn business and doing nothing.*

What pissed you off more? Was it the hue of my skin or the fact that your daughter didn't take your advice to "adopt kids from some kin in the family"? I guess I'll never know. I would say that we will talk when I get to Heaven – but I refuse to believe that they would open the Pearly Gates for someone like you. What I will say in closing is what that five-year-old couldn't: Fuck you and your coins.

Katrina

I analyzed it, over and over again. The therapist was wrong. I didn't feel better; it still belonged to me. I needed it officially released – returned back to the iniquity from whence it had come. I located an envelope, addressed it to *The Grandmother,* and sealed it shut. No stamp, no return address – I walked to the corner and placed it in the slot of the mailbox. I can just about imagine the reaction of the postal worker who haplessly opened the mailing and received that profusion of poison.

Selfishly though, liberating this unwanted possession generated some sense of contentment. And even if the correspondence lay dormant, unread, in a pile of refuse, it was still one less bag I slaved to carry.

Chapter Eight

That night I dreamt that I was a guest on the *Oprah Winfrey Show* – the theme of the segment: Reuniting Biological Families. I shared the stage with a diverse sampling of adults who had been given up for adoption and listened as they relayed the tragic events of their lives. I made no contribution to the forum. I, ego-tripping (as usual), had no desire to expose my family's clandestine intimacies on national television. Although the other adoptees held my empathy, the pity that would be garnered from the viewing audience was something I had no use for.

What the hell can you do with pity? I'd much prefer another's understanding of how it feels to come into contact with strangers – on the train, in the mall, at the grocery store – whose facial characteristics so closely mirror yours, that you'd like to say, "Hi, I'm so sorry to bother you. But the resemblance between us is uncanny.

I was wondering if you could possibly be my mother (or sister, or grandmother, or aunt, or cousin)?" But the urge to do so must be resisted because it defies the personality traits of a sane, well-mannered person. I'd also rather someone, who wasn't getting paid, have an earnest interest in hearing the contents of an oppressed soul that has been ill-treated for no reason other than simply existing.

But pity? I can't do anything with pity. So when the hostess coerced me into speaking, I lied. I fabricated a tale of having a great relationship with both my parents and that I had been blessed to have been adopted by such a loving couple. I guess part of that is true. I woke up before I had the opportunity to meet the woman waiting in the green room, who had traveled all the way to Chicago for an introduction to the piece of her that had been missing for so long.

In reality, at this point I can't honestly say that I would welcome an encounter with my biological parents. I suppose it would be nice to look into the faces of those responsible for my conception – but then what? Do we hug and kiss and cry and catch up on forty-one years? How would I refer to them? Surely not as "mother" and "father." Good, bad, or indifferent, those positions are already filled. I'm sure my cynicism regarding this topic is directly connected to the resentment I've harbored against two people, whom I desperately searched for, who weren't searching for me.

Can you imagine looking for someone who doesn't choose to be found? It's far more daunting than the proverbial endeavor to locate a needle in a haystack; it's a chore that requires someone (such as myself) to sacrifice his/her meager financial, physical, and emotional resources in exchange for a maybe. Maybe you will find them; maybe they will be happy you've found them; maybe you will gain a bit of peace once they've been found.

I am no quitter; I have stuck with various enterprises long past the expiration date of a sour venture. Yet, in the case of the missing sperm and egg donors, my role as 007 ended after all leads had gone frigidly cold, and I made the executive decision to allow them to remain at large rather than utilize any more of my reserves to hunt down Bonnie and Clyde. At a point of hopelessness, I did ask my father for any possible clues he could grant me in solving the mystery, but he pled the fifth and directed me to interrogate my mother.

My mom would be the ideal accomplice with which to commit a crime: poker face, hard to break, and when all else fails (rather than confess) she would concoct such a distortion of the actual events that by time the authorities figured out they'd been bamboozled, you and she would be in the South Pacific sipping Mai Tais.

Mom told me that when my biological mother became pregnant with me, she was fourteen years old and her mom thought it best for her to hand me over to another couple, rather than ruin her future and her (and her family's) reputation by having a child out of wedlock. So the girl was sent to south Jersey to live with relatives until she gave birth, which is how and why I was born in Salem County. Mother further purported that my birth-name was Pamela Clarke.

The final element that she creatively wove into this masterpiece of fiction was that I was adopted through a private agency, and although she didn't think it to be in my best interest, there was no possible way anyone (including

> *Have you ever seen the movie* The Usual Suspects, *in which the character Roger "Verbal" Kint a.k.a. Keyser Soze does no less than a brilliant job of eluding the FBI agent by feigning his recollection of the events in question? All the while the tale he is spinning is based on various tidbits of information, which are visible on the agent's bulletin board.*
> *Absolutely love that movie, but the real-life version isn't quite as entertaining.*

me) could ever unseal the confidential birth files; it was an agency policy.

I have no idea where my mother's inspiration sprang from in the manufacture of her deceit. Nor have she and I ever discussed why she felt the need to mislead me. But her ruse ended my search. It was disheartening to come to terms with letting it go, yet based on my mother's information, there was no need to continue to torment myself.

Sometime after the manhunt ceased, I learned the truth; Mom had lied. I guess it doesn't matter how I found out, and if it did, I couldn't say anyway. In honor of the plea-arrangement between my informant and me, the confidence will forever remain in the restaurant at which it was disclosed. The rebuttal to my mother's falsehoods were offered quite matter-of-factly – post my directing the server to return the steak that was far too pink to be considered medium-well, and prior to the three shots of brown liquor that tempered the new knowledge that burned my chest. Irrationality tempted me to make a mad-dash for the exit to seek-out and confront Mother. Sensibility though, held me captive in the booth for a good while after the nark tenaciously protested my request to be left alone and eventually bid me goodnight.

I remember sitting at the crowded bar, fingering the rim of the empty glass, lost in disbelief, unconscious of the presence of the other patrons. I needed to think rationally about what I had just learned. For me, everything is about principle. I could forgive and understand Mother's disloyalty if I believed that the act had been committed for my benefit. Perhaps this was mother's way of shielding me from the disappointment of continuing the wild goose chase, or what I could possibly discover at its end. Or maybe this was her way of protecting herself – her bid to selfishly have me know only one mother.

I could conceive no definitive way to solve this enigma. In order to adhere to my vow to protect the identity of the innocent, I couldn't ask. All hell would break loose if I presented her with this information. This was complicated by the fact that with Mother, I was never certain of her motives. I resolved that the matter would be best left alone, as there may have been a good reason to abandon the search. If it was self-serving, I did not want to hurt my mother by giving her the impression that I sought her replacement; I just hoped to find these people so that I could gain some enlightenment as to who I am.

A satisfactory substitute for the truth regarding my

biological parents would have been an understanding of who Mother was and what made her tick. Yet, I did not comprehend her pain, nor did she, mine. Often, it's virtually impossible for another to emphatically view your experience through their lens. The only way for another to have a thorough understanding of your experience is for the viewer to see it in the same manner and context as you do. Otherwise, their interpretation is tarnished by their own experiences and biases and beliefs and perceptions.

If it were possible to lend Mother my eyes I would have. And it would've helped tremendously if I had been able to borrow hers for a while. Regretfully, neither of us ever accomplished the feat of seeing the world as the other saw it. At the time of her death, we were somewhat strangers to each other – never understanding the other's intentions related to some deed – yet never hesitating to perform those deeds that were most significant.

One of the most challenging acts that I was ever charged to perform for my mother's sake, was the drafting of her obituary. It forced me to admit that I had spent all of my life in the company of someone I did not know. I'm uncertain whether she purposely built an impenetrable wall around herself, or whether she desired to allow others into her space but didn't know how to do so.

But I yearned to be close to her. I wished to spend Saturday afternoons, at long lunches, listening to stories of her childhood, and the first boy she kissed, and high school dances, and her migration to New Jersey, and her and Daddy's courtship, and how my brother and I were selected to be her children. I needed to share the "period talk" and the "boy talk" and the "becoming a woman talk" and all the other discussions that assist in progressing a girl through childhood, a teen through adolescence, and a young woman into womanhood. Instead, I had those conversations with girlfriends, who more often than not, knew about as much or less than I did about the topics. And left ill-advised on matters consequential to my development, I took it upon myself to unwittingly experience the ways of the world – the results of which, unsurprisingly, were often indicative of the blind leading the blind.

There were, in fact, surrogate mothers who checked my periodic waywardness and offered guidance. Yet as much as I will always appreciate their mentorship, it was never quite enough to compensate for what was deficient in the relationship between mother and me.

Our rapport was similar to my relationship with The Grandmother. I feared my mother and knew full

Chapter Eight

well the consequences of crossing her. Her tongue was both biting and scathing; and her hand was no less treacherous. Mother could denigrate you to a point that you wished you could evaporate into air. Her wrath was mostly saved for me, but my father and brother caught hell as well. Outsiders were exposed to a warmer person than we lived with. But no one was safe from her fits of fury.

That is not to say that my mother had no good qualities; she had many. When she chose to, she was sweet and kind and giving. And although she could terrorize me, no one else (excluding her family) could even contemplate the thought of doing so. I've heard her declare, on many occasions, "I don't care if I got them out of the garbage can! They mine, and you'll go through me to fuck with them!"

I've never understood it. I have seen my mother go to war for me, but then turn around and abuse me. What do you call that? Love? Pride? Is it the willingness to die for someone whom you choose not to live for? Or granting protection from having a blade plunged in another's back, unless it is by your hand? Is that the same as the bitch (no pun intended) who will fight to the death to protect her litter, but will not hesitate to kill and eat every one of her defenseless pups? These concepts are unfathomable to me. Yet, the acts of loving another, how we internalize and process love, and what that act looks like when it is executed – may very well be the most complicated of all human endeavors to understand.

I believe the complexity in the relationship between my mother and me stemmed from her critics' disapproval of her decision to provide a home to two homeless babies. This was further challenged by her desire to remain in good graces with her family. She had a fear of sacrificing established relationships with them in exchange for forging unsecure ones with the newcomers. It was difficult for her to make all those pieces fit nicely into one puzzle. Concessions had to be made; there was no way around it. She wasn't granted the autonomy to love us all at the same time. So, the two outside guests suffered – especially the little yellow girl who was way too damn smart and feisty and mouthy for her own good.

To my children, though, she was a saint; they had the fortunate opportunity to a have grandmother who adored them. My children received all of her attention and affection that was denied to my brother and me. I wonder if that was her form of atonement, meant to equalize the scales of malevolence bestowed upon me.

Or if, perhaps, it had more to do with the fact that she was free to love them without the repercussions of judgment or disparagement from others. Or maybe, more simply, she was older and wiser, and having witnessed the damage that withholding love can do to a child, decided it was best to give hers liberally to them.

I must admit that at times I found myself envying my children. I hadn't had a mother or grandmother with whom I could snuggle in bed – or laugh and joke with while preparing a meal – or share my secrets, fears, and dreams with.

Nonetheless, I was happy for them. They would not be vacuumed into the vicious cycle; my mother, apparently, had a dysfunctional relationship with her mother; I had one with her; and I pray it stops here. I am working on ensuring that it does; I truly am. That is why my conscious would not allow me to keep them away from her after Daddy died, and I was called the "adopted daughter," and I was instructed to keep my distance from the home where I grew up. I did, foolishly, forbid them to have any contact with her for three months or so. But watching my babies connive and conspire to secretly communicate with their grandmother was enough to convince me that their well-being was more important than my pride. They never knew that I was aware of their *Mission Impossible* antics; I guess it never occurred to them that I was the one viewing and paying for the long distance phone bill.

When I fully surrendered to the triumvirate and took them to visit their grandmother, I remained in the car during drop-offs and pick-ups. I had not yet arrived at a stage of forgiveness that would permit me to venture beyond the safety of my vehicle, open and pass through the gate and stroll up the walkway. And based on the reports of my children, especially the younger two who were not yet old enough to discern which information would be best left at Momma's house, my mother was no closer to redemption than she had been on the day Daddy left us.

I was outraged that she would speak ill of me in the presence of my children. They would listen to her on the phone, vilifying Mommy to her sisters and girlfriends. And they, out of their allegiance to me, would attempt to defend me. Often I was tempted to reinstate the restriction policy, yet not only was it previously unsuccessful, but it made no sense to involve my children in an adult mess. And it was quite messy. I reasoned that both my mother and I were vital elements in their existence, and hopefully they could have both of us without being made to choose a side, which I don't believe they ever did.

In time they learned to manipulate the situation to their benefit, quite the way children are able to play two parents who are never on the same page: Mom says no – I'll get it from Dad, and vice versa. In our case, it was usually I who denied the request of financing some item that I believed they could do without. Typically, *their Momma*, who never felt the need to seek my opinion in such matters, satisfied these solicitations.

It went on like this for the next nine months. There were times I made it half way through dialing Mother's number or managed to turn the engine off and step one foot out of the car while delivering her grandchildren; but my fear of how she would receive me aborted these impulses. So I remained, a motherless child – mostly in an inebriated state that provided little comfort in the way of pacifying my reality.

I had two new assistants: the morning drink that helped to take the edge off facing a new day, and the evening drink that helped me relax. In truth, my assistants needed to be fired; their job performance sucked. Once the drunken state has subsided, all those things you hope to ignore and/or forget are still prowling about. And to make matters worse, the false feel-good from the truth serum is likely to facilitate some words and/or actions that cannot be easily erased the morning after. But I continued to mix and mingle with these acquaintances – even after I realized that our toxic friendship needed to end. But I had no one else – just them.

Of course, I could always find someone to vent to; drama sells. But at the end of the day I still found myself holding onto all this stuff. And even if I could find a sympathetic ear, at 2:00 AM who was willing to endure my ranting, most likely I wouldn't express those things that remain deepest hidden in my spirit.

So no one knew that I was becoming a semi-functioning alcoholic – and that I was losing my resolve to live – and that I feared that I would die like that. And that although I did complain of it, no one truly knew the depth of the hurt I felt when I found out my mother and her nephew had done some slick shit with Daddy's insurance policies and investment accounts to prevent my brother and me from receiving a penny from his estate. I knew what Daddy had; I was the only one who helped him complete his paperwork.

I calculated that Mother was brewing some nonsense when she asked her nephews to dig through Daddy's documents, while sending me off to do house chores, but I never thought my mother could ever stoop so low. I could have had both of them prosecuted for fraud.

Chapter Eight

Instead, I spent many nights – void of sleep – sipping, pacing, and cursing the day that this bitch picked me out of the lineup, only to bring me into bullshit. That's what I wanted to tell someone: that I hadn't asked for this shit – that she had come and got me – that I had busted my ass for as long as I could remember just for this woman to mouth the words, "I'm proud of you," - and that I've already repaid and repaid and repaid my debt to her for providing some whore's throw-away with shelter.

But who could I tell who would understand that? I needed someone to comprehend that I didn't care about that money; everything my father had given me during his lifetime was sufficient. I was good with that. My dilemma was that Mother would not remove the butcher knife that she had rammed into my back so many years ago – and my greatest fear was that she would continue to twist and turn the thing until so much of my blood exited the wounds, that there would be no possible way to revive my life.

Chapter Nine

Mother spent the first Thanksgiving after Daddy passed with her partner in crime and his family. I hadn't seen her in months, and the last gashes were just scabbing over. It humored me to envision my mother and her nephew sitting around the dining table. My brother though, who rarely expressed his views about mother, condemned her more than he ever had.

I sympathized with his frustration, and I missed the family tradition that we had become accustomed to sharing on this day – but for some reason, my mother and her nephew's buffoonery (now) tickled the hell out of me. Not that I found it amusing that these two had heisted my dad's life savings, but for far better reasons. One: there is no honor among thieves. And as soon as her nephew had swindled all he could from her, I doubted there would be any more invitations to share a holiday meal.

The two of them had never been close. As a matter of fact, Mother would talk shit about him, horribly. She didn't like him – and most likely, he didn't like her. But they shared a common ground on two fronts: greed and self-centeredness – a dangerous combination. And I knew it wouldn't be long before they exploded. Two: My mother thought she was hurting me, but she wasn't. I had already come to terms with her absence from my life. I resolved that I would love her from a safe distance but I would never again get close enough for her to push the blade in further. And Three: Karma is a Bitch. I feel the need to say that again, Karma-Is-A-Bitch. And when you least expect it and it is most inopportune, that bad energy that you have sent out into the universe always has a way of finding you. And when it does, you receive far worse than what you put out.

I am not in the habit of wishing harm on anyone. Nor did I wish harm to come to Mother or her nephew. But I knew that their enterprise would not end well.

In early 2008, Mother and I began speaking again. I don't remember the exact day or specifically who initiated the conversation or why. Over the course of the next two years we saw and/or spoke to each other when it was necessary. Speaking and/or being in the other's presence was usually attributed to something involving the children. Very rarely did I enter her house; it was attached to far too much bitterness that I was determined to shield myself from.

I did, in fact, ask my mother if the children and I could stay there for a while after I was laid off from the vice principal position in 2009. Her response: "The kids can come, but you'll have to find somewhere else to go."

I had neither a job or the prospect of one; I had no substantial savings; I had no one to ask for money; and even though my landlord and I had a pretty good rapport, I knew that it wasn't a good enough relationship for him to allow me to live there for free. It had taken me days to build the courage to make that phone call; and without hesitation, she shot me down.

Luckily, by the end of the summer, I was hired for a teaching position and was able to make it through the situation without being evicted.

In reflection, I am grateful that she did not allow me to stay at her home. She knew that there was no way in hell that she and I could peacefully co-exist under one roof – not at that juncture on our journey. But there would come a time when we would live together again. And it would not be at my request or hers. It would be at that point, in the scheme of things, when it was meant to happen.

In all the years I've spent in church – of all the sermons I've lent an amen to – all the scriptures I can quote – and for the culmination of hundreds, if not thousands, of hours spent on my knees in prayer – it still remains to me an absolute mystery as to how, when, and why God moves. But if I know nothing else, I know for certain that it was He who placed his hands on my mother and me – f or twelve days – until we were healed.

It began under the guise of a curse rather than a blessing. The scenario with Daddy was materializing again: same symptoms, same diagnosis, same time frame, and the same ending. The major variance: unlike Daddy, Mother did not want my help and fought me to stay out of her affairs. I would do no such thing. She was the only mother I had ever known, and regardless of our past, there was no possible way I would desert her.

I saw Mother more frequently in the final year of the four years between the time Daddy was given his wings and she received hers. I returned to teach in Newark, and she lived only a short distance from the high school where I worked. Some mornings I called and offered to bring her breakfast. Mostly she declined the gesture. Here and there she would request a small cup of French vanilla and a plain stick. Upon delivering her coffee and doughnut, our morning chats were identical in context.

"How much do I owe you?"

"Mom, you don't owe me anything; it's fine."

"You better hurry up before you're late."

"I'm going; have a good day."

She usually included an additional commentary as she held the screen door ajar and studied me as I scurried down the walkway; whether it was about my hair or my skin or my outfit or me needing to lose weight or gain weight – the critique was typically unpleasant. I grumbled profanities during the entire ride back to school; but it was her way and I dismissed it until the next time I saw her.

When I began a doctoral program in September of 2010, she picked my daughter up from school and kept her at her house until I got out of class. Every Thursday evening I called when I reached the parkway exit near her home and Mom and I would talk for the next ten to fifteen minutes until I pulled up outside. I used most of those brief conversations as a forum for which to complain about work or school or how both were wearing me down.

She offered neither solace nor comforting words for my troubles; it seemed that I was speaking aloud to myself with the benefit of having the availability of a silent ear. Often her response was limited to five words: "You're stronger than you think."

At the time, I thought this was mother being mother – and providing a retort that was both ambiguous and detached from human emotion. I realize now that her statement was both clear and heartfelt. Maybe she knew a great deal more about me than I had ever given her credit for. Possibly, she knew more about me than I knew of myself. But I rejected her sentiments as sincere because of our history in which I perceived myself as the weak one who was surrounded by giants such as her and The Grandmother, whose validation and pride I sought, but was never good enough to attain. So I took her comment as yet another factious attack, believing that the words were meant to discredit my character as opposed to providing encouragement.

But soon, the depth of her knowledge about me would reveal itself. More so than this, I did not realize then that we were walking through the door and into a space that was designed to prime us for redemption and forgiveness and wholeness. I would assume this is why the future is an entity that remains a mystery to us. Had I had a hint as to what awaited her and me in the concluding three months of her final year, I am sure there were many things I would have made every attempt

Chapter Nine

to alter. There were moments that required every bit of my being to drudge through. There were numerous incidents that exacerbated the internal conflict that was erupting in my soul. There were situations in which Mother embarrassed, demeaned, and dehumanized me – when all I was trying to do was help. But now, in reflection, I understand why things happened the way they did, and if I had to do it all over again, I wouldn't change a single thing.

I vividly remember the expression on my mother's face when the oncologist gave her the results of her lab tests. The doctor told Mother that the cause of her weight loss and stomach pain was stage four pancreatic cancer. Her diagnosis was less of a shock to me than mother's reaction. She sat there; stone-faced, no emotion, glaring straight into the eyes of the accuser who had just pronounced her death sentence. Mother analyzed her for a while, as if the two were engaged in a game of chess, and the next intricate move would determine the outcome of the rivalry. I spectated from the sidelines, obliged to convey no palpable tinge of fear or weakness.

I wanted to embrace her or say something. I did neither. Instead, I battled my humanness, and re-directed my gaze to the doctor's medical degree that hung on the wall behind her desk. As I sat transfixed, awaiting mother's retort to her opponent, I prayed the schooling represented by the fancily-framed educational document had trained this *specialist* to deal with the likes of Mary Register – because Mom was about to make her prove that she was worthy of every letter in that title.

When the match resumed, mother spoke very curtly and direct.

"What can you do?"

"There is very little that can be done, Mrs. Register. The cancer has metastasized to your liver. Surgery is not a feasible option. But we can try chemotherapy, which may prolong your life."

"How much time?"

"With the chemo, perhaps six months. Without, I believe we're looking at half of that."

"And you know this how? You think you're God?"

"No, Mrs. Register, I don't profess to be God. Based on my experience I –"

"Damn you, your experience, and some damn chemotherapy! The only one who knows when I'm leaving this earth is God – and since you ain't Him, I'm done with this meeting!"

"I understand how you feel, but –"

Chapter Nine

"You understand how I feel about what? You got some doctor telling you that you got cancer and you about to die? 'Cause if you don't, you don't understand a damn thing!"

"Mrs. Register, I apologize. That's not what I meant. I'm simply trying to say – "

"Don't waste your breath. Nothing else to listen to. Let's go, Trina."

"I truly didn't mean to upset you so badly. On your next visit maybe we can – "

"Next visit?" Mother laughed. "You must be crazier than you look! I said, let's go, Katrina!"

The stalemate was over. There was no victor; it wasn't possible for there to be one. I just hoped that we could make it out the door without security being called in.

For fear that my eyes would apologize for my mother, I avoided looking at the doctor. Mother had been both rude and disrespectful to this woman who was only trying to do her job. But she was grown – and right or wrong, Mother was entitled to deal with this in her own way. My apology would say that I was judging her. Who am I to magistrate how anyone should counter being told that he or she has ninety days to live? So, when mother snatched her arm away as I tried to help her out of the chair – I fell back. On the way out of the office, when she demanded that the doctor answer the question, "And just how do you know my daughter?" - I fell back. When she refused to speak to me on the ride to her house – I fell back.

I felt so sorry for her, for my children, for myself. I knew she would spend each of her remaining moments fighting with herself, with me, and with doctors. But I hoped, for her sake, that she would dedicate some portion of her remaining days to making peace with all those things done, and all those things that would forever remain undone. But the next month would find mother in a worse space, and more malicious toward me than she had ever been.

The first incident occurred after I had requested prayers for my mother on a social networking site. Somebody told somebody, who told somebody else, who eventually called my mother. About two weeks after receiving the diagnosis, the telephone rang. It was long after midnight. I answered the phone, half asleep, and was greeted by this question:

"So you want me dead, do you?"

"Mom?"

"You tellin' people I'm about to die – but I got a trick for you and that doctor you put up to sayin' I got cancer. I ain't goin' no damn where!"

Chapter Nine

"Let me get this straight. I got the doctor to *make up* that you have cancer? Are you serious? Why the hell would I do that?"

"Cause you think you gettin' something. You ain't gettin' shit. Not a damn dime!"

"Holdup, I –"

"No, you hold up, hefa! You ain't got the power of attorney! I changed the will your father had, and I changed the beneficiaries on all the accounts! You and that fake-ass doctor you workin' with can wish me dead if you want! Y'all both can kiss my black ass! Cause you ain't gettin' shit from me, bitch!"

She was still screaming when I disconnected the call. I didn't think it was possible, but she was knifing deeper this time. Could she really believe that I would have someone deceive her into believing that she had cancer? Did she really believe that I was so vile that I would do such a thing?

I cried hard that night – so much so, that by the end of it I had developed a new resolve: those were my last tears. I was resolute in my decision to help Mother through to the end of her journey, but I was detached from the emotional side of it. I would handle any required task – but the thick skin that I hadn't developed in forty-one years ripened overnight – and I vowed that this was my exodus from the role of weakling that I had become so proficient in playing.

So on the afternoon when Mother was unresponsive to my and my brother's phone calls and our pleadings for her to open her apartment door, I ignored her as she cursed me and dealt quite tactfully with the rescue squad and police officers who had to climb through the windows of her home to get her out. And the next week at the hospital, in front of a full room of visitors, when mother declared, "I should spit in your face," I excused myself from the room, pulled myself together, and did not hesitate to sign the home hospice papers that were presented to me by the oncologist later on that evening.

And a few days later, after the medical transport personnel transferred mother from the hospital to my home and she refused to speak to me, I dismissed her actions and began the daily routine of bathing her, brushing her teeth, moisturizing her body, combing her hair, dressing her, feeding her, administering medication, and empting the catheter bag as if I were a well-trained medical professional. I was focused. She could curse me, call me names, and refuse to speak, if that was what she chose – but my mission was to care for my dying mother – and given that I was already well acquainted with this treatment from Mother, it was going to take a hell of a lot more than ugly words and the rolling of eyeballs to deter me from my goal.

I was grateful for the two hours that the hospice nurse came each weekday. She provided additional assistance and care, tips on how to manage tasks with greater ease, and a brief respite, which allowed me to run an errand or take a nap. The remaining twenty-two hours each weekday and all day Saturday and Sunday were my responsibility. It almost made sense why Mother did not want to provide in-home hospice for Daddy. But just as with Daddy, I couldn't place my mother in a nursing home. That is no indictment against nursing facilities, or those who must place a parent or loved one there. For me, it simply was not something I was comfortable with. I would be lying if I claimed that the undertaking was easy; it was daunting and overwhelming. Even prior to mother coming to my home, there were times (from the onset of the awareness her illness) when I wanted to scream, "Are you fucking serious? Can you see me trying to show you that no matter what you do or say, I'm still your daughter? I'm not going anywhere; I'm right here! Can't you see that I won't abandon you? Don't you know how much I love you?"

I guess she didn't trust me enough to believe any

of that. Yet her convictions, at this point, were of no consequence to me. I didn't have anything to prove to her or anyone else anymore. That in and of it self is ironic, because I had spent my entire life attempting to prove *something* to her. I was her daughter and she was my mother – period. We didn't share the same blood or facial features, and her relatives had never been mine, nor would they ever be. Even though an immense distance separated us, and neither of us had the skills or tools to abridge it, I refused to permit past hurts or the present ones to dissuade me from making my mother's last days on this earth as comfortable as I possibly could.

During the twelve days mother spent at my home, I wore many hats: I was nurse; I was hostess to visitors; I was comforter to my children; and I was the sole point of contact for the doctors and the hospice medical personnel, social worker, and clergyman. I believe mother witnessed what I was doing and fully opened herself to me for the first time in my life. It took a few days, but the look of anxiety eventually disappeared from mother's face. The stage of her illness restricted her ability to say much, but she began to look at me and respond with the shake of her head, and managed a pleasant expression when I conversed with her. In her room, I played gospel songs that I thought she'd like to listen to. Her favorite was Hezekiah Walker's, "I Need You to Survive."

I would play that song, over and over again, until she and I tired of humming and singing. And then I held her hand and we sat in, what others would assume, was silence. But for mother and me, it was more communication than we had shared in forty years. Likewise, most evenings, I slept on the small loveseat next to her bed. I would awaken to find her smiling and staring at me. At first, I wondered what she was thinking – but soon I didn't question it. There was love and peace in her eyes – things I had not seen there before. It filled me with joy and forgiveness and redemption – and I was no longer a motherless child.

On Sunday, May 1, 2011, I was awakened from my catnap by mother's loud groans. Her breathing was hampered. She paused for long periods of time between breaths and eventually gasped for air. Mother was struggling to remain in the company of the living, characteristic of the spitfire she was, the strongest woman I have ever known. I knew the end was upon us even before the nurse came, checked her vital signs, and ushered me into the kitchen where she draped her arm around my shoulder and concluded her monologue with, "You did all you could do; allow that to give you some comfort."

When she left, I did not escort the nurse to the door – I accepted our final hug at my dining table. I had grown fond of her in those twelve days. I would miss the talks we shared over cups of tea; yet I understood that the nature of our association was business, and our business was done. After she left, I returned to mother's room. I played our music and stroked her hair. She did not hum that day, nor did I sing. Mother was preparing for a new journey; one in which she would join Daddy and her relatives and friends who had gone on home ahead of her and now eagerly anticipated her arrival. I was bracing myself for goodbye.

I let the guardrail down on one side of her bed, positioned my head on her shoulder, and pondered all of it. This woman, from whom I had moved an hour away to separate myself from – the one who had a chokehold on my existence from its inception – was leaving now, and I wished she could stay. We were no longer strangers. We loved and trusted and had faith in each other now. We could now share those sunny, Saturday afternoons and fill them with long – awaited conversations and laughs and smiles. But God gave us twelve days to fix it, to make it right; to clear the muck and mire that had rooted deep within our spirits. And we had accomplished that. There was nothing more in this situation that I could ask of Him. So, together we listened to our song a few more times. The last time her chest dropped and failed to rise again. I bid her a pleasant voyage to her resting place. Then, hoping that her soul was still close enough to hum with me, I sang our song: *I Need You to Survive.*

Chapter Ten

I might end this portion about my mother and me there. She and I had made our peace – and it was a beautiful, joyous, and tranquil space. However, my intuition strongly advised me that the curtain had not yet closed, and it was premature to take my final bow. I deduced that the snake that had been lying dormant, smelled money, and would be slithering his way back for an attack. But I wasn't five years old anymore. Screaming, crying, and begging Daddy to come to my rescue were not available options. So I mentally geared up – metaphorical pitchfork in hand – and if he came for my neck, I was ready, willing, and equipped to take off the reptile's head.

He had showed up at the hospital a few times – looking uneasy – sitting around – ear hustling – asking questions. Mother had said very little to him. In fact, the relationship between her and the nephew had taken a turn for the worse when she demanded that he repay the money that she had lent him. Apparently, he was under the impression that her generosity was a gift and not something that required reimbursement. Of course, there were no more invitations to share holiday pleasantries and turkey and cranberry sauce after the first invitation. And by the time, his frequent visits with Mother had subsided to an occasional telephone call, in which they gossiped about his brother's, sister's, and other family member's affairs, Mother was talking about him as badly as he was everyone else. The final straw was when he invited Mother to attend his son's wedding ceremony – but not the reception. He said he couldn't afford to have more guests come.

With as much money as she *loaned* this cat over a three-year period, he tells her she is not invited to a reception that she probably helped to finance. Mother never relayed this information to me; my brother did. As much as I would have enjoyed gloating in her face, I allowed it to remain a secret between Brother and me. I actually felt sorry for her – more like pity than sympathy – the two of which, in my estimation, are not synonymous.

Pity has a negative connotation, which usually comes

> Now ain't that some shit?

Chapter Ten

from a place of guilt or shame. For example, how many times have you gone through the drive-through of a fast-food restaurant to be greeted by some random person standing by the pick-up window begging for money? You say, "I'll buy you something to eat, but I'm not giving you any money."

He or she says, "I can go and get my own food."

You know good and damn well that the money would not be used for food, and the only thing he or she is hungry for is that next quick fix. But something (pity) compels you to give the money anyway, because you may feel guilty or shameful for not helping the person.

Sympathy, on the other hand, is when you have an understanding of another's plight and offer sincere sentiments. Like when a co-worker loses a family member and you sign a group card and donate money toward a collective gift.

All of that is to say, I would have felt guilty for laughing in mother's face after the nephew played her. I knew it would come to that. And although she was a willing participant in the corruption, I despised the fact that some low-life had taken advantage of my mother. Maybe she had let it ride because he was her blood – but he wasn't mine.

I understand that the act of vengeance belongs to

the Lord. I also agree with the notion that when one seeks vengeance, he or she is required to commit an act that is as evil, or worse, than the initial offense caused by the perpetrator. I wasn't looking for revenge – revenge would force me to relinquish my power – my thoughts and actions would be at his mercy. I needed to be strategic. Allowing anger and bitterness to guide my course of action would result in my demise. I couldn't do anything about what had previously transpired, but going forward, this was my game and would be played according to my rules.

I had questioned the nephew while mother was in the hospital, not because I believed he was man enough to reveal the truth about having extorted money from my family, but because I needed to figure out exactly who I was dealing with.

The nephew had lied in my face, which meant that not only was he a coward, but also that the clown was ruthless enough to conceal his part in the wrongdoing, even as my mother fought for her life. I tried to convince my brother that the nephew was not to be trusted. But brother and I were cut from two different cloths. We were raised in the same home, but our experiences were worlds apart. He was brown and he fit in, and no one questioned his belonging to the Register clan. Brother

Chapter Ten

developed relationships with the cousins that I was not privy to. They were his kin. They were my enemies, who would ignore and ostracize me when I attempted to join in a game – tease me until I was in tears – pinch me until the blood rose to the surface of my skin – satisfy their lust by inappropriately touching and fondling and prodding private places – and threaten to injure, or even worse, if I ever mouthed one word of it to anyone.

So when Brother could not be persuaded to stop providing the nephew with information, I understood. Unlike mother, he did love us all at the same time, I did not question his allegiance to me, but I feared his need to continue to belong to them. Yet, this was merely a minor snag in the ensuing battle that I would use to my advantage. I could not tell Brother about my scheme – but he and I would play good cop/bad cop. And, although

> Robert Greene's The 33 Strategies of War # 13 – KNOW YOUR ENEMY: The target of your strategies should be less the army you face than the mind of the man or woman who runs it. If you understand how that mind works, you have the key to deceiving and controlling it. Train yourself to read people, picking up the signals that they unconsciously send out about their innermost thoughts and intentions.

the thought of using Brother as a pawn in my plan was mortifying – I was not betraying him. If all turned out the way I calculated it, he would ultimately appreciate the end result of this deception.

The nephew had a few tricks left up his sleeve. In his mind he had pulled off the first heist, and his greed and arrogance would not permit him to remain content with that. I was mindful of this, which is why I contacted an attorney during the first weekend of mother's stay at my home. Everything that Daddy had worked so hard to provide for his family would not be forfeited to this bastard.

With my children, Brother, and sister-in-law present as witnesses, the lawyer first questioned Mother as to her desire to grant me power of attorney and name me as the executor of her estate; then she ensured that Mother was not being coerced into making this decision. Mother verbally answered these questions, and it was the first time she had spoken since she had arrived at my home four days earlier. Finally, the lawyer asked for mother's permission to allow me to guide her hand in signing the documents; Mother agreed. Then she looked at me for a long time, as if to say, "I'm trusting you, don't disappoint me." I had no intention of doing so.

The day after Mother passed, the first bombshell fell

on Brother: Mother had, in fact, removed him and me as beneficiaries on the insurance policy that Daddy had purchased and maintained for her for over thirty years, and replaced us with the nephew. Watching Brother attempt to hold back his emotions lacerated my core. I would've confided this to him the week after I first contacted the insurance company – but I could not disclose it. I was clearly at odds with the nephew – and I needed Brother to remain amenable with him for as long as necessary. The cat was out of the bag now. At the funeral home, in the company of strangers, Brother hung his head in the disbelief that he too had been conned by the nephew. When all was said and done, I would make it up to him. I would help him navigate through all of this – the way he had always helped me. But for the moment, the plan was incomplete. For now, I would perform my role as the inane, emotional, pathetic fool the nephew presumed me to be. I must say my theatrics were impressive.

I behaved as though the funeral director's information sent me into a state of distress. Brother invited the nephew to join us. I realized that I needed him to consent to releasing a portion of the $50,000 policy to cover the funeral expenses, so I refrained from challenging his presence there. Instead, I protested his participation in the meeting – but I rationalized (actually counted on) the fact that he could hear us from the opposite side of the thin wall that separated the office from the vestibule. With the appearance of a lunatic, I wildly ran out of the room, screaming at and cursing the nephew. Brother, of course, was right on my heels to restrain me from physical contact with the snake. I carried on so badly that Brother was forced to throw me over his shoulder – kicking, swinging, and screaming expletives – and lug me out the entrance door.

Once I got to my car, Brother rested my weary frame against its side, and stood guard in front of me – seemingly shielding me from all the wickedness that existed in the world. As expected, the nephew, now believing that he had complete control of the situation, appeared in the parking lot – smirk on face – yelling, "You better tell that little bitch something! She better show me some respect

> *Robert Greene's The 48 Laws of Power*
> *# 21 – PLAY A SUCKER TO CATCH A SUCKER- SEEM DUMBER THAN YOUR MARK: No one likes to feeling stupider than the next person. The trick, then, is to make your victims feel smart – and not just smart, but smarter than you are. Once convinced of this, they will never suspect that you have ulterior motives.*

Chapter Ten

or I ain't signing shit!"

While pretending to make a break from Brother's grasp and screeching some additional profanities, I let brother steer me into my driver's seat. The funeral home director soon appeared. I could see from the rearview mirror that she was coaxing the nephew to return inside. Next, she walked to the car and presented her appeal to me:

"I know this is a challenging situation and I feel for what you are going through. But I'm sure you want to provide a decent going-home ceremony for your mother. You have every right to make those arrangements, and I promise you that you will. If you will allow me to work out the financial side of this with your cousin, you and I can meet later on today to make the necessary preparations."

(The re-mix of what she said was: I need you to take your crazy ass away from here long enough for me to make my money from this dude.)

I hesitated before responding, as if she had presented me with an extremely difficult challenge that required the use of my mind, body, and spirit to figure out.

"He's not my cousin," was my first response.

"I understand that. But he is the person who has control over releasing the insurance policy to the funeral home," she gently stated, as though I might be too fragile to totally absorb the dilemma.

"How much of the policy can I use to bury my mother?" I questioned, as if I didn't already know the answer.

"You will be free to spend as much of it as you like. Once he releases the policy he cannot dictate the cost of the funeral. But he will receive whatever is left over," she responded, as lightly as possible, so that perhaps I wouldn't realize that she was about to make a shitload of money from this deal (but better her than him).

"When do you get paid?" I inquired, needing to know exactly when I could crush and destroy my opponent.

"I'm sorry, I don't understand the question."

(Like hell she didn't).

"I'm asking you, at what point in this process is the payment to the funeral home final and can't be retracted by him?"

"When the services are complete," she advised, eying me suspiciously.

"And when are they considered complete?" (I had to be certain).

"Once the casket is lowered into the ground."

I paused again, this time clutching the steering wheel and placing my forehead at its top.

"Okay," I mumbled, as if conquered.

"I will call you later, once I am ready for you to return. Until then, please try to remain calm. I know this is hard for you, but God always has a way of working things out."

I gave no response.

After she left the parking lot, I looked up at Brother, who had been listening from the other side of the open window. I read his eyes; he felt bad for me. I wanted to tell him to save his sympathy for what I had in store for the nephew. Instead, I asked if he was staying and he shook his head, yes.

This worked out well; it would provide the nephew with time to apologize to Brother and provide some feeble excuse for having not been upfront when questioned about the change of documents. I knew my brother; he was far more trusting than me, but he wasn't an idiot. The nephew, digging his own hole, was worth far more than anything I could have said about him. I also needed Brother to remain at the funeral home, because the nephew would be forced to present his representative, and wouldn't be able to pull any fast ones with Brother around.

Mother's funeral was fit for royalty. I hand picked a

magnificent casket: ivory with gold etchings and a silk lining. The director suggested that I purchase the floral arrangements from a florist with whom she contracted. I ordered so many flowers that there was barely room to fit them all in the front of the large sanctuary of the church. I endeavored to spend every penny of the insurance policy on the funeral. The thought of this loser walking away with money that I'm sure mother would rather have seen used to fund her grandchildren's college funds tormented me. In the end, he still managed to take over $20,000. God would deal with him and his ill-gotten gains, but as soon as the casket was lowered into the ground, all bets were off between him and me.

I would give them no tears. Mother's family had contributed to enough of my sorrow. Our finale would be exceedingly different from what they had come to expect of me; they would witness the personification of strength. I was a rock.

On the night of the viewing, I cordially greeted Mother's friends and colleagues as they made their way to pay their final respects. Brother kept asking if I was okay. He wasn't sure what to make of the smile that remained plastered on my lips. Mother's family kept their distance, but I felt their eyes on me as they congregated and dialogued in muted tones.

Chapter Ten

The following morning I rose early. I sat with a cup of green tea, in front of my desktop, drafting a few words I needed to say about my twelve days with my mother. Having cleared it with my brother and children, I telephoned one of the deacons to inform him that I would be the only one speaking during the part of the program where acknowledgements and words of condolence were to be offered. They, her kinfolk, had said enough and done enough during her lifetime. Today, they would have no say. They would hear expressions that were representative of those who truly loved her.

I wore white. Mother was dressed in white as well; she appeared to be a peacefully-sleeping cherubim. I was determined to make my angel proud of me that day. I did not falter in my objective to be strong – even as I could hear the sobs of mourners as I read our tribute to her – even as I kissed her forehead before closing the casket lid – even as the pastor spoke fondly of mother during the eulogy – even as I observed the pallbearers carry the finely constructed metal frame to the site where the shell of who she once was would forever remain buried – and even as the casket was lowered into the earth.

The nephew rode in a limousine reserved for him and the relatives. I thought it quite ridiculous, but it was his money he was spending to look and feel important.

As we traveled back to the repast, I leaned over and whispered to my brother, "It's done. He's not coming in."

Brother examined me for a moment, and then shook his head in agreement. Then I provided our limo driver with explicit directions regarding "the tallest man, in the third limo, with the …" The driver assured me that he would have security take care of it. Brother pleaded with me to go directly inside the church once we parked. He said, "If some shit pops off, I'll handle it; you've done more than your share." I smiled at the authority with which it was said, and offered no rebuttal.

Brother, a few of his friends, my son and my ex-husband joined the repast about half an hour after the driver helped us out of the limo. It was taking so long for them to come in that I began to get worried. When they finally strolled through the banquet hall doors, laughing, I knew that all had worked out well – or at least well for us.

Brother reported that it had gotten quite ugly for a while. The nephew had refused to "accept this treatment" and had rallied the troops to storm the door. Brother continued relaying the events – smirk on face – stating how the nephew had asked him to take a walk with him and had tried to get him to sell me out by telling him that he intended to give my brother a share of what was left of the money if Brother agreed to "handle your sister."

That's when brother had reached his boiling point. He had told the nephew, "There are two ways you can leave – in your car or in a body-bag. If I were you, I'd take the first option so that the funeral home isn't spending what's left of the money on you."

The nephew left brother standing there, obviously opting for the opportunity to spend his gains in good health. Then, like the sniveling coward he was, he had lied to the relatives, telling them that none of them would be allowed inside. After making sure that everyone who could hear them knew what they thought of me, they left. Brother and I laughed so hard we both had tears running down our faces. When we finally got it all out, he leaned in close to me, kissed me on my check and said, "I'm proud of you baby-girl."

Before I could ask, "For what?" he said, "I know what you did, Ms. Slick. You got that one off."

I hugged him and cried with my head buried in his chest for a long while; at last it was safe to release it all. When I finally ended our embrace, he looked at me through teary ears, and whispered, "Thank you."

Now, I thought about turning from the airport bar to tell Coach everything that had happened: how I had taken care of Mother for twelve days and had experienced a joy and peace that had never before been mine; how I had handled the nephew and the relatives and proved to everyone that I could be strong – and how I had managed to do it all without picking up the phone to ask for his advice or guidance or comfort.

But I didn't say any of that. Thirty seconds, or so, had already passed since his initial approach. Maybe he wasn't standing behind me anymore – and if he was, perhaps he would just walk away and leave me be.

Book Three

On Learning to Smile

Black
Woman
Urban
Inner-city born and raised
College-graduate
Yet educated in the streets of Newark
Stripped
Of an indigenous language, culture, religion, identity, and home.
Home
Where is my home?
Where am I welcomed?
Is there anywhere on this earth that my dark presence is welcomed?

Anger
Hopelessness
Helplessness
And Despair
Tell me. Why should I smile?

The Conspiracy
To mis-educate my children – to disenfranchise my sisters – to un-employ and under-employ my brothers –
And to make all of us believe
That somehow it is all our fault.
The conspiracy – has been a major success.

And I'm drowning, dying, losing consciousness in my anger, hopelessness, helplessness, and despair.
Tell me. Why should I smile?

The ghetto teaches you to
Look tough
Walk tough
Act tough
Think tough
On a festive occasion
Or when something amusing occurs

You are allowed to smirk or laugh
But to Smile
A Natural,
Warm,
Cordial,
Soulful,
Smile,
That, was never taught to me.

Recently I met a woman, an Hispanic woman
And it struck me as odd
That she had this Smile.
I mean, she had this Smile that was
Natural and
Warm and
Cordial and
Soulful.
Upon meeting this Smiling woman, I foolishly thought to myself:
She looks like me, but she's not like me.
She's obviously one of them –
Or she believes she is anyway.
But upon talking to her and learning the stuff behind the Smile, I found that she was very much like me.
Her rage, her anger, her pain

Were all like mine.
But she had learned to
Channel it,
To defy it,
To overcome it,
With a Smile.
A Natural,
Warm,
Cordial,
Soulful,
Smile.

She smiles because her grandfather, for whom she was named, could not smile.
She smiles because the ghetto, los barrios, is void of smiles.
She smiles because the racist world attempted in vain, to confiscate our smiles – and so she figured if she could teach one of the warriors to Smile, in spite of it all – then she had struck a mighty blow against the system that had systematically stolen all our Smiles.

Que mujer mas bella.
Gracias Anna, por ensenarme a sonreir.

What a beautiful woman.
Thank you, Anna, for teaching me to Smile.

Chapter Eleven

RepresentativeBook – Status Update:
Today, marked the end of sixteen years of serving as an urban educator. I wish
to thank the hundreds of students who allowed me to play a role in their lives during that time.

To my students I say: I pray that something I said or did, assisted in enabling you to find the wisdom, courage, and strength to navigate your journey past the confines of the poverty, crime, dependency, and gang warfare that has become indicative of our home city. Be exceedingly more than this. Be "The Rose that Grew from Concrete." Be well and blessed.

I Love You.

Nov. 18, 2011 / 2:51 PM / Near Newark, New Jersey

Six months after my soul began to breathe new life, and the pieces of me that had been scattered for so long began to gravitate to the center to form the wholeness that I had endlessly sought – I was fired from my job. The story of it is easier to relay now that two months have passed since it happened. In a nutshell: a student threatened to "fuck" me; the new principal was derelict in her duties to address the situation; and after I informed the teacher's union of this matter, which in turn brought it to the attention of the principal's superiors, I supposed they convened in a clandestine meeting and came to the conclusion that it would be in their best interest to fire me, rather than risk the possibility of exposing the inexperienced *school leader's* incompetence. The termination letter provided no explanation

> *Why would an employer allow someone whom they intended to fire, to report to work? It's funny, they thought to call a substitute to cover my classes, but didn't believe it necessary to contact me. What would you call that? Would that be someone attempting to embarrass and/or make an example of the poor sap? Or to show exactly has the power? SMH. Power in the wrong hands can lead to destruction.*

Chapter Eleven

for my removal, other than to say that the district was exercising its rights to remove a non-tenured teacher, "at any time and for any reason."

At some point, I would receive compensation for the thirty-day notice, (that they were required to provide) in lieu of working for the next four weeks. And just like that, it was done. Without the privilege of being forewarned, I reported to work that Friday, and was greeted by one of the vice-principals, who regretfully made me aware of the decision.

Perhaps, if this event had transpired a year ago, I would have given in to the urge to locate the principal, argue, make a scene, and maybe even get into it so badly that security would have had to get involved. Don't get me wrong, I was beyond pissed, but I had overcome far bigger battles with far more formidable contenders than this chick. If it made her feel like the big girl on campus to wield her perceived power to hurt others, then that was her right.

Of course, by the nature of human emotions, I wasn't quite so reserved and diplomatic in my opinion of her sixty days ago. But armed with the experiences that helped to create the new and improved *Grasshopper*, and the assistance of a few dear friends who advised me that this was a blessing in disguise; it didn't take very long to get past this bump in the road. I refused to waste time feeding it more energy than it deserved.

There are two things that I know for certain. One: God has not brought me this far to leave me. Two: Any hole that anyone has ever tried to dig for me, is one in which they, themselves, ended up falling into. So I was good. I would miss standing in front of a classroom, engaging students – as they listened to my attempt to bring life and meaning to the words of Maya Angelou and Toni Morrison and Arthur Miller and Baldwin and Hughes and Shakespeare and Poe and Tupac and Frost. I would equally miss being a sounding board and an advisor and a surrogate mother and a resource facilitator and wearing all of the other the hats that come with a commitment to being an urban educator. Even so, I understood that it was time to move on to a different phase of the journey, perhaps in a new direction, to try something a little different.

For almost two decades I had served children well, and it was simply time to move on. In actuality, my loyalty to that calling would have kept me stagnant in that place, suffering under the principal's domain – so I have nothing but gratitude for *Ms. Leader* for serving as the mechanism instrumental in assisting me with forward motion.

Chapter Eleven

I must admit that I was a bit lost the following Monday morning. When the alarm clock sounded at 5:45 AM, I rose to begin my usual workday routine. It didn't dawn on me until midway through taking my shower that there was nowhere to report to, no time clock to punch in, and no students to teach. I stood there, allowing the tepid water to soothe the tension in my bare back. But my old demons were attempting to surface – causing me to feel as if I had failed the three who depended on Mommy to assure that they wouldn't miss a meal and provide shelter and keep the heat, hot water, and electricity on. What do I do now?

I turned the faucet off, wrapped myself in a towel, and went into the kitchen to locate some familiar comfort. There were a number of bottles of liquor left over from the Labor Day barbecue I'd hosted at the end of the summer; until now, they had sat dormant. A number of times, I had thought about giving or throwing the alcohol away. Very seldom did I drink now, and when I did it was limited to one or two cocktails or glasses of wine in a social setting. But something had to get me through this first day. I placed the pint of cognac and a shot glass on the countertop of the center island, and positioned myself on one of the high stools. The microwave clock read 6:18 AM. "Its noon somewhere,"

I said aloud to myself.

As I began to fill the glass, I received a text on my cell phone, which had been left on the dinning table. *What now?* I wondered as I reached to retrieve the message. The communication was from my prayer partner. It read:

I woke up with you on my mind. Please remember, He is with you now, as He has always been and will always be. You are not alone ... You once said that the 23rd Psalm is your guiding scripture. Dig into your faith and let that scripture guide you.

My hands shook, uncontrollably, as I lay the phone down on the table. I grabbed the half-full glass and slung it with all my might, causing it to shatter on impact against the wall, its brownish contents defacing the chiffon colored paint. Seconds later, I could hear the heavy footsteps of my daughter. She stopped at the entrance to the kitchen.

"Mom ... you okay?"

"I'm fine, baby – I'm fine."

She didn't believe that and neither did I. She disappeared and returned with the broom. I motioned for her it hand it to me.

"I'll do it. You go get dressed for school."

She hesitated, finally turned to walk away, stopped

after a few steps, looked around and said, "You don't have to get me anything for Christmas. I already have everything I need."

She left me slumped on the floor. I rose and poured the contents of every bottle down the drain. Then I got on my knees, in the middle of the kitchen, and talked to Him.

"The Lord is my shepherd; I shall not want.
He maketh me to lie down in green pastures; He leadeth me beside the still waters. He restoreth my soul; he leadeth me in the paths of righteousness for his name's sake. Yea, though I walk through the valley of the shadow of death, I will fear no evil: for thou art with me; thy rod and thy staff they comfort me. Thou preparest a table before me in the presence of mine enemies; thou anointest my head with oil; my cup runneth over. Surely goodness and mercy shall follow me all the days of my life; and I will dwell in the house of the Lord forever."

Chapter Twelve

RepresentativeBook – Status Update:
On this day, I am so very grateful for my parents, John and Mary Register. From my father, I learned the importance of a strong work ethic – the significance of honor, loyalty, and commitment – and how to tell a good story and share a good laugh. From my mother, I was afforded strength, determination, and perseverance. From both, I was taught the infinite power of humbling myself and getting down on my knees to thank and praise and converse with my Creator.
Happy Thanksgiving All! Enjoy your loved ones today and everyday!

Nov. 24, 2011 / 7:03 AM / Near West Orange, New Jersey

I remained in bed all day. A number of friends had invited the kids and me over to share in their holiday dinner, but I had respectfully declined the offers. My children were with their fathers, which was a first for a holiday, as I had been in the habit of monopolizing *special* days. But I had put up no argument this year. In fact, I was eager for them to spend the day with their paternal families. I was in no shape to entertain anyone.

A few days before Thanksgiving, it had occurred to me that there would never again be the aroma of mother's cooking – or the instructions as to how much gravy to add to the corn-bread stuffing, or the amount of milk to mix in the baked macaroni and cheese – or trudging, in silence, through the wee hours of the morning to cut and chop and grate and stir and blend the ingredients necessary to create her famous dishes. I missed her terribly. I'm sure a psychologist could write volumes in regard to the dichotomy of the relationship between mother and me.

We loved hard – and we hated just as intensely. We protected each other from outside forces, yet we inflicted injury on each other. I guess it's fair to say that ours was certainly one of the most functionally dysfunctional

Chapter Twelve

relationships that two people could experience. And yet, I still longed to be in her company on this day. I thought about how drastically different the image of us would be sitting around the dinner table – imparted with the knowledge that we now had of each other. I smiled at the mental picture.

Chapter Thirteen

RepresentativeBook – Status Update:
HAPPY NEW YEAR!

Jan. 1, 2012 / 8:22 AM / Chelsea Piers, New York

I had let my girlfriend talk me into attending a Black-Tie Affair with her and her husband the previous night. Spending New Year's Eve, dateless, as the third wheel, made me feel pathetic (to say the least). But, it had been my only invitation for the evening, so I had gone along for the ride. I hadn't put my usual effort into dressing for the occasion: simple black cocktail dress, light on the make-up, and hair carelessly twisted up into a bun. I had thrown on my *get-somewhere-and-sit-down stilettos*, because I figured I would do more sitting than standing. Boy, was I wrong.

He said he noticed me when I first entered the

ballroom; I didn't see him until he sat in the empty chair across from me at my table. I thought he was strikingly handsome and very well put together, but after the initial onceover I turned my attention back to watching the party-goers on the dance floor. There was a time when all I did was dance, but the love of it had dwindled after daddy had died. I itched to join them, but instead I sat bobbing my head to the rhythm of the song.

I'm not sure how many times he said, "Excuse me," before I realized he was speaking to me. When I eventually acknowledged him, he pointed at me, then pointed at himself, then pointed at the dance floor. That was cute. I smiled a little, but shook my head no. His entire aura had Coach written all over it. And I was determined to avoid anything that looked, acted, or smelled like him. Thanks, but no thanks!

I got up and went to find the rest room; I figured I'd remove myself from the table long enough for him to focus in on someone else, and long enough for me not to reconsider his offer. The line to get into the ladies' room was ridiculously long, so I aborted that plan and went out to the rooftop courtyard. I interrupted a couple that were in desperate need of a room, a backseat, a park bench – anything other than the wall they were leaning against with dude's hand hiking up the bottom of her gown. My presence didn't stop them though, in fact, I think it may have heated things up. Freaky!

I was in no rush to return inside and the view of the harbor was beautiful from up there, so I ignored the two love-birds and gazed at the water from the farther side of the patio. The weather was brisk; I wished I had grabbed my coat on the way out. A short while later, someone came up behind me and placed a suit jacket over my shoulders. I turned to find him standing there, cigar in hand, smiling.

"Did you follow me out here?" I naively asked.

"Sweetie, you're cute, but you're not that cute. I came out to smoke." He'd replied with one of those I'm a smart-ass grins.

"Thanks for the jacket, but I don't need it," I said smugly, wanting to punch him in the side of his head.

"Well, I don't make it a habit of imposing myself on a lady, but from the way you were shivering, I would say that you are definitely cold."

I said nothing, just leaned against the railing and studied him a while. If I didn't know any better, I would swear that this man was Coach's twin: same personality, same mannerisms, same boldness, and same (contradiction of) humble-arrogance.

"Can we please get out this cold and go dance, or

are you one of those sisters with no rhythm? I saw you bopping your little head up and down; I didn't want to be the one who told you, but you were completely off beat." He said this looking me directly in my eyes – without the slightest inclination that he might be joking.

"Are you challenging my dance skills, sir?"

"My name is Justin – Justin Holland – and yes, I am absolutely challenging your dance skills, Ms." He gestured his hand to shake in introduction.

"I never turn down a formidable challenge, Mr. Holland," I retorted as I shook his hand.

"That's good to know, Ms. Lady – whose name I hope to find out by the end of the night."

"Maybe you will; maybe you won't. Depends on what your skills are – your dancing skills that is," I mischievously commented with a wink, as I past him on the way inside.

We danced straight through the last two hours of the party. At some point I came out of my heels. Mr. Justin was quite a character – interjecting jokes and wise cracks as we enjoyed each other's space. After the DJ played the last song, we walked together to the table to retrieve our things.

"I'm not ready to leave you yet, Katrina," (I had disclosed my name by the end of the third song. What can I say? He had skills.) he said, while helping me put my coat on.

I looked up and gave him one of those – the cookie ain't that easy, brotha – looks.

"I'm not trying to get in your panties, Ms. Lady; I like your company and I'm not ready to go home yet. Can we go have a cup of coffee?"

"I don't drink coffee and it's two in the morning."

"Well, I'm sure you drink *something*. And this is New York City; we don't sleep."

The man with all the answers; how could I turn him down? I followed him to a diner nearby. We talked for the next five hours. I learned that he was an urban-native, had worked his way up the ranks in law-enforcement and played golf at least twice a week (Coach's secret, long-lost brother). He spoke as one who could maneuver both a board meeting on Wall Street and a conversation with the fellas from his hood on the corner. We flowed. It was cool. In the last hour he said:

"I like you, Katrina, and I enjoyed you this evening, or should I say this morning. But I want to be honest and tell you that I have a special friend, and as much as I would love to get to know you better, you're not the kind of woman that I would want to mislead."

He confessed it as if the weight of the world had been

released from his broad shoulders.

"Well, what kind of woman would you mislead, sir?" I questioned with a wide smile, anxious to hear the response.

"The kind that wouldn't care about lying down with me tonight with no strings attached tomorrow … and you're not her," he answered rather candidly.

"Oh no? And who exactly do you think I am, Mr. Justin Holland?"

"A woman who deserves to be loved. Doesn't take a wise man long to figure you out, Ms. Lady. You're intelligent, you're beautiful, and that shy smile says that you have a good heart that's been hurt before."

"You met me seven hours ago and you're confident that you know all that?"

"I saw that you were physically attractive when I first I saw those skinny legs walking into the banquet hall." We both laughed. "I confirmed the inner beauty part by the time we were wopping to Eric B and Rakim." More laughter. "Aside from the fact, that it's my job to read people. I'm sure there are some other little niches to you, but you're not hard to profile. You got this tough, little feisty exterior, but that's not you inside." (He had me pegged; I sat there grinning).

"Why did you approach me if you have a *special

friend?"

"You want the truth?"

"Yes."

"Because you remind me of her and I haven't spoken to her in about two weeks."

Ain't that some shit. I remind him of her and he reminds me of Coach.

"That may very well be the same reason that I'm sitting here with you; you remind me of someone who was very special to me ... but we haven't spoken in a year."

"Are you serious? Damn, that's funny. So you're using me, Ms. Lady?"

"No more than you're using me, sir."

Long laugh.

"Why aren't you and your friend speaking?" I inquired.

"Because she's ready for a committed relationship and I'm not so ready."

"Do you love her?"

"Absolutely. I just don't know if she's the one that I want to spend the rest of my life with."

"Why is that?"

"I'm not sure. She's a good a girl. And there's not a lot about her that I would change."

"So, it's you."

"I guess you could say that. It's possible I'm a little scared."

"A brotha who legally carries a gun – scared?"

"Yeah, and that better be kept between us or I will find you in New Jersey!"

"Your secret's safe with me, Mr. Holland."

Another long laugh.

"Maybe instead of continuing this conversation with me, you should be heading to where she lives."

"Is that right, Ms. Lady?"

"I believe so, sir."

We look at each other for a while.

"I think I'm going to take that advice, right after I take care of this bill and walk you to your car."

"Oh! You actually listen to someone? I didn't include that as part of your profile."

We laughed some more on the way out of the door. I smiled the entire ride home thinking: *that was a good start to the New Year. I needed that.*

RepresentativeBook – Status Update:
Katrina and Justin Holland are now friends.
Jan. 3, 2012 / 3:19 PM / Near West Orange, New Jersey

Chapter Fourteen

RepresentativeBook – Status Update:

This week, forty-two years ago, a young woman gave birth to a baby girl. For reasons unknown to me, the woman decided to give the child up for adoption and never had the chance to hold, or feed, or play with, or clothe the baby. Although I have never seen her face or heard her voice, she is of great significance to me. And so, I dedicate this birthday week to her, for allowing me the opportunity to live.

Jan. 16, 2012 / 8:48 AM / Near Newark, New Jersey

Sometimes I catch myself staring at a stranger with similar facial features. I still wonder where they are and what their lives are like, but the malice toward them is gone. I'm uncertain as to when it happened, but the contempt I held for my biological parents dissipated into something akin to a strong fondness. Especially, for the young woman who carried me for nine months and placed me in the arms of a couple who was better equipped to provide care for me.

I owe her a debt of gratitude for that. Having carried three children to term, I can't imagine how it feels for a woman to be separated from a child after having gone through morning sickness, doctor visits, and the little jabs and kicks from the bundle inside. Wherever you are, I appreciate you! I thank you for giving me life. It hasn't been all good – but it's been all mine. And the longer I live, the more I am grateful for it.

Chapter Fifteen

I will be spending my birthday on a plane en route to San Francisco. A close friend that I attended college with asked if I would be interested in putting the story of my life in writing. I laughed when she first suggested it; who would want to read about my life? But she was relentless. Every time we spoke on the phone or communicated on *RepresentativeBook* she brought up the book idea.

I finally surrendered. So I in three days, I will be boarding a plane to travel across the country, to have someone delve into my soul and pick my brain. In one sense, it's kind of exciting. I've always wanted to write a book. I just never figured that I would write one about myself, which leads to the other side, which is the scary part. If I write about myself and my life and my family, I am putting myself way out there to be judged by others. The thought of it makes me feel more vulnerable and transparent than I'd like to be. It's not like writing on *RepresentativeBook* – *or* another social networking site; you can pretty much say whatever you want and present yourself to be whoever you choose. But with a book that's autobiographical, most of that is the truth; you are on candid camera. Not sure if I'm ready for that.

And what if we spend all this time writing, editing, and publishing a book that no one ever reads? But then again, perhaps the end result is less important than the process – the journey to the outcome. I guess we will see. If nothing else, I will certainly have a great time in San Francisco!

RepresentativeBook – Status Update:

Often we are in pieces. We give and sacrifice and forfeit bits of ourselves to the people who and the time when and the places where … Becoming whole is a process.

One can never be certain of the hour or the day it will happen. But the moment when all that stuff is released from your spirit – and you arrive at a solid awareness that whatever your situation or position in life may be – you are good with just being you – is when you have transcended to wholeness. I Am Whole.

Chapter Fifteen

Katrina (the artist formerly known as Grasshopper).

Jan. 22, 2012 / 6:02 AM / Newark Airport, New Jersey

I figured the brief snowstorm would cause some delays to my travel plans that day, but I hoped to arrive in San Francisco early enough to join my girlfriend and her family for 11:00 AM worship service. I hadn't stepped inside a church in quite some time. That day, my birthday, would be as good a day as any to rekindle the feeling of fellowship. But from the looks of things in the airport, I knew that the return of the prodigal daughter might end up being postponed until the next Sunday.

After checking my bags, stripping down at the security check and reporting to the gate to find that my flight would be delayed for two hours, I headed to the only open restaurant in the terminal, which was packed to capacity with travelers who were being inconvenienced by the aftermath of the weather. I spotted a man getting up from a seat at the bar and sprinted to secure it. After ordering a glass of cranberry juice, I contemplated which details I should share with Marie, the aspiring author. As my mind scanned its memory book, I concluded that there would be no point in sharing any of it, unless I relayed all of it completely and honestly.

And then his voice lured me away from my reflections. And, as I sat in disbelief that Coach and I could end up in the same airport, in the same place, on the same day, at the same time – I hesitated to respond to his greeting, because I wasn't certain whether I was prepared to face him. But after a minute or so had passed, I was confident that I was. I turned to find him, still standing behind me. I looked directly in his eyes and began to speak.

"You knew I was weak. You knew I was vulnerable. You knew I needed someone. And you took advantage of me. I don't know if that makes you a bad person or an opportunist or a womanizer or a bit of all of them … I'm not sure … I don't know who you are."

"I'm your friend Grasshopper."

"My friend? Friendship is a full time job; you worked part time, and only when it benefitted you. But you didn't do anything to me, that I didn't allow you to do … and it took some time, but I forgave myself first, and then I forgave you. And I'm –" I paused to listen to the announcement:

"Flight 042 to San Francisco in now boarding at gate twenty-two."

I gathered my bags and turned to face him again. "I'm not Grasshopper anymore. That person left a while ago; she's not coming back."

Chapter Fifteen

We stood there, both of us knowing that this was our goodbye. He leaned in, kissed me on my forehead, and said, "Take care, Katrina."

I shook my head and responded, "Peace and blessings."

And then I walked out – smiling. And I didn't look back.